Bolt
Cou

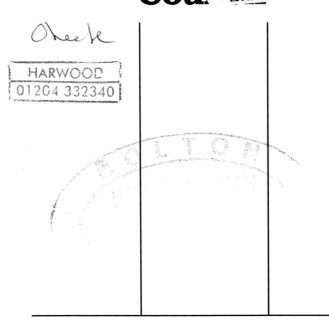

Please return / renew this item HO
by the last date shown.
Books may also be renewed by
phone or the Internet.

Tel: 01204 332384

www.bolton.gov.uk/libraries

Quigley's Way

A dying man, Peter Barker asks Sheriff Quigley to deliver a message to his family. Quigley does so, only to find himself the target of range baron Huston McRae, who controls everything in Gila County, including the local sheriff, and doesn't want an outsider nosing around in his affairs. And above all, he doesn't want Quigley helping Noreen Barker, Peter Barker's widow.

When McRae's attempted intimidation of Quigley fails, he orders him killed. Quigley sends for his deputy, Murray Fishbourne, and together they take on the local sheriff and the gunslingers McRae sends after them. But as the fighting intensifies, can Quigley and Murray survive?

Quigley's Way

P. McCormac

A Black Horse Western

ROBERT HALE

© P. McCormac 2018
First published in Great Britain 2018

ISBN 978-0-7198-2703-7

The Crowood Press
The Stable Block
Crowood Lane
Ramsbury
Marlborough
Wiltshire SN8 2HR

www.bhwesterns.com

Robert Hale is an imprint
of The Crowood Press

The right of P. McCormac to be identified as
author of this work has been asserted by him
in accordance with the Copyright, Designs and
Patents Act 1988

*Half a century ago a wonderful woman agreed to be
my wife. Thank you Ruby.*

Typeset by
Derek Doyle & Associates, Shaw Heath
Printed and bound in Great Britain by
CPI Group (UK) Ltd, Croydon, CR0 4YY

1

Sheriff Joshua Quigley put his heels up on a chair and stretched his long lean frame, and yawned widely. In his mid-twenties, Quigley had a square face with a close-cropped dark beard. The sheriff picked up the *Idlereach Chronicle* and shook out the pages. As he began reading he thought he heard distant gunshots and sat up straight.

'Goddamnit,' he muttered, looking towards the door.

The shots came again and Quigley got to his feet. Grabbing his gunbelt he strode across to the door while at the same time buckling the rig around his waist. The rig held twin holsters with matching Colt single-action army revolvers.

As the lawman strode down the street in the direction of the gunfire a few men spilled out of the Joy Juice saloon and scattered into the street. The sheriff changed direction, ducking down an alley. He quickened his stride and eventually came up behind the Joy Juice where he found a few men standing in the yard.

'What's going on?' he growled.

'Sheriff, thank God you're here. It's Todd Sloane has kicked off,' a grizzled old-timer told him.

'Yeah, got in a row with some cowboy,' a man in a fancy waistcoat told him.

Quigley recognized him as a dealer from the saloon.

'Sloane!' Quigley shook his head in disgust. 'I guess he's been drinking then?'

'Came in last night and started,' the dealer told him. 'He's been drinking ever since.'

'What about Greg?' Quigley asked. 'Couldn't he deal with it?'

Greg McGurk was the owner of the Joy Juice and a man usually able to handle any trouble in the saloon. They were interrupted by shouting from inside and a few more shots blasted out.

'McGurk's lying behind the bar with a slug in him. Don't know how bad he is.'

'Damnation! Anyone else hurt?'

'That cowboy got one in the gut,' another man said. 'I saw that afore I cut out.'

Quigley bowed his head momentarily, and taking a deep breath walked to the rear entrance of the saloon.

'Careful, Sheriff,' the dealer cautioned. 'Sloane might be drunk but he's still dangerous.'

'I reckon Sloane's more dangerous when he is drunk,' the old-timer added. 'Don't seem to slow him down none.'

Quigley was thinking this was an occasion when he could have done with his deputy to back him up. But that was just wishful thinking. Deputy Murray Fishbourne had gone to Templeton visiting his mother. This was one crisis the sheriff would have to sort out on his own.

Carefully he pushed the door open and stepped into the passageway leading to the bar-room. The door at the end of the corridor was ajar and Quigley peered through the opening. He spotted Sloane behind the bar, hatless, with one hand resting on the neck of a whiskey bottle. A pistol was lying beside the bottle. In Sloane's other hand he held a second weapon.

The gunman was wearing a topcoat buttoned at the neck, leaving the bulk of the garment gaping to reveal a dirty shirt that may have been white once but was now yellowing and grimy. It might have been an easy shot for the sheriff to draw his Colt and attempt to put a bullet into the troublemaker from his vantage point, but that was not Quigley's way. The lawman brushed his fingers against the walnut grips of his holstered Colts and then stepped cautiously inside the room. On entering the barroom, Quigley held his hands out in a non-threatening way.

Todd Sloane spotted the movement and swivelled his weapon towards the lawman, his eyes narrowing as he spotted the newcomer. Quigley flinched as the weapon came to bear on him. Maybe the lawman was born under a lucky star, or maybe because of some whim working on Sloane he didn't pull the trigger, and Quigley breathed freely again.

'Sloane, what's this all about?' Quigley said, his voice surprisingly steady for one who had been a hair's breadth away from being plugged. 'How come you shooting the place up?'

'Goddamn Sheriff Quigley!' The gunman held his gun steady on the lawman. 'I wondered when you'd show up.'

Quigley shrugged his shoulders.

'Well, I'm here now. You going to put that gun down and tell me what this is all about?'

Now he was inside the room the lawman could see people cowering on the floor, gamblers, drinkers and saloon gals. One man lay curled up near the front and blood had leaked into the sawdust.

'Let these good people continue with their fun,' he continued. 'You and me can maybe have a drink and talk this over.'

A small trickle of moisture worked its way down

Quigley's back.

'Come on over and join me,' Sloane suggested. He beckoned with the whiskey bottle. 'You and me have some jawing to do.'

The gun never wavered, the muzzle aimed squarely at the sheriff. He could see the end of the barrel like a black eye glowering malevolently at him. It would take very little to set Sloane off, and he would pull that trigger and at this distance he would be unlikely to miss. Quigley stayed where he was.

'Sure thing, Sloane. Just put the gun down and we can jaw all night if you're so disposed. It makes me mighty nervous when someone aims a gun at me. It's mighty unsociable of you to invite me for a drink while holding a pistol. Almost like you were threatening me if I didn't take up the offer. You know what I mean?'

Sloane bared his teeth in what might have been an attempt at a smile, but it came across more like a snarl. Without taking his eyes from the man confronting him he raised the whiskey bottle to his mouth and sucked at the liquor.

'You remember Stonewall Faulks?' he said when he took the bottle from his mouth.

'Stonewall Faulks!' The cold sweat was almost a rivulet as Quigley repeated the name. 'Rings a bell somewhere. Mayhaps saw it on a poster or something.'

'He had his cousin's name of Golay.' Sloane did that grotesque grimace. 'Well, Blane Golay has come all the way here to Idlereach to meet you.'

Quigley knew, then, what this was all about. Todd Sloane was a wanted man. Quigley could have taken him in anytime. But up until now Sloane had committed no crime in Idlereach, and Quigley had just kept a cautious trace on the gunman when he learned he had arrived in town. While Sloane behaved himself, Quigley left him alone. But now it was becoming clear that Sloane's arrival in Idlereach was no accident. Two notorious gunmen in his town meant only one thing: they had come to execute the man who had shot and killed Stonewall Faulks.

2

'I'm a reasonable man, Sloane,' Quigley said. 'Why don't this Blane Golay come forward and introduce himself?'

But Quigley had already spotted the gunman. While everyone else in the saloon cowered on the floor, one man was still sitting at a table. The sheriff had never seen Golay before, only on wanted posters. The gunmen had obviously planned their ambush thinking Quigley would come in the front entrance. If he had come in that way he would have been in a crossfire between the two gunmen. Coming in at the back had left Golay unsighted.

There was no doubt in Quigley's mind that the men had lured him in here with one purpose only. It had been Quigley who had shot Stonewall during an attempted bank robbery. And Sloane and Golay were here for revenge.

If Deputy Fishbourne had been available one of them would have come in the front door while the other came in the back. But now Quigley was in a tight situation with only his own wits and resources to help him survive. Sloane took another slug from the whiskey bottle, his eyes never moving from his prey and keeping his gun aimed squarely at the lawman. Quigley smiled ruefully.

'I guess this Blane Golay ain't much of a sociable man. Probably some hillbilly punk from the backwoods that speaks in a dialect nobody can understand excepting his ma, who was probably a sow anyhow. Most likely he don't even know who his real pa is, there were so many hogs gathered in the ditch around her. Come to think on it Sloane, are you related by any chance? I can smell you from here.'

Sloane's eyes widened in stupefaction at this diatribe. There came the scraping of chair legs as Golay, obviously stung by Quigley's insults, scrambled to his feet. Sloane's eyes flicked sideways towards his partner – and Quigley threw himself back through the door which he had left open behind him. Shots blasted out as the man behind the bar fired into the doorway, the bullets passing harmlessly overhead.

Quigley now had both his Colts out and was crouching inside the corridor counting the shots. There was a pause in the shooting and the lawman plunged back into the bar-room, his right-hand revolver firing at Sloane who was in the action of picking up his spare weapon on top of the bar. One bullet caught the gunman in the shoulder and spun him around and he crashed against the shelves behind him, bringing bottles tumbling down. At the same time Quigley's left-hand gun fired off shots towards Sloane's accomplice.

Bullets hammered into the wall beside the lawman as he moved further into the room blasting away with both guns at two different targets. He dropped flat behind a table, one gun already pouched and with practised fingers reloading the other.

There was an eerie silence within the saloon and then

the sheriff caught movement behind the bar. His aimed his gun but did not fire. Slowly he stood: the saloon owner, Greg McGurk, was leaning heavily on the bar top. There was blood on his shirt. He gave a lopsided grin at Quigley.

'Where's Sloane?' the sheriff asked.

'He's lying here with your bullet in him and a lump on his head.' McGurk hefted a baseball bat. 'I couldn't resist the chance to get my own back, so I clouted him after you shot him.'

Quigley walked across to the place where he had last seen Blane Golay. The gunman was crumpled up in the sawdust. The sheriff knelt beside him and prodded him with the barrel of his gun. It was only then he noticed the wound in the man's scalp, where one of his bullets had parted his hair and left a raw track. All around the saloon, customers were stirring now they reckoned the danger to have passed. A chorus of voices broke out.

'Goddamnest thing!'

'Jeez Sheriff, that was some shooting!'

'Did you see that? Took on both at once.'

In the midst of the hubbub Quigley walked across to the bar and looked critically at the blood on the saloon owner's shirt.

'How bad is it?' he asked.

'Hurts some, but I'll survive.'

'Sheriff, this man's badly wounded,' someone called.

Quigley turned to the man kneeling beside the cowboy stretched out on the floor.

'Lay him on one of the tables,' McGurk called from behind the bar.

Three men carried the cowboy to one of the gaming tables. They were surprisingly gentle as they did so. McGurk had a whiskey bottle out and was filling two glasses. He pushed one towards Quigley.

11

'Here, I guess you'll need that.'

Quigley threw back the drink and kept his face upturned with his eyes closed.

'We live to fight another day,' McGurk said sombrely.

'I guess. Anyone sent for Doc Reardon?'

Quigley had to raise his voice to be heard above the excited babble of voices as men came back indoors and discussed the shootout.

'Sure thing, Henri Oakley's gone to get him.'

'I need some men to help me carry these two hoodlums down the jailhouse. I don't want them coming to and causing any more trouble.'

Quigley was kept busy for the next while, supervising the removal of the wounded men to the jail where he searched them for hidden weapons. Both men had knives, and Golay had a hideout gun, all of which the sheriff confiscated. The prisoners were lodged in separate cells and locked in.

'Tell Doc when he's finished with McGurk and that cowboy to come on down here and tend the prisoners. Anyone got a handle on the cowboy?'

None of the men present knew the name, and Quigley dismissed them. For long moments he sat down in the seat where only a short time before he had been peacefully reading the newspaper. Eventually he got up and went and got out the box where the wanted posters were kept, and went through them until he found the one on Golay.

'Humph!' he grunted. 'Five hundred dollars for Golay, and five hundred for Sloane.'

Quigley settled back to read the paper, thinking when Doc Reardon discovered his two patients were worth $500 apiece he would up his fees considerably, meaning there would be less for the sheriff to collect.

The prisoners come to at some stage while the sawbones worked on them. They cursed and swore and painted lurid descriptions of what they were going to do to Quigley.

'You ain't gonna die easy, Quigley. You'll be staked out on an anthill with bits sliced off you.'

'I'm gonna cut out your heart, you son of a bitch.'

Doc was none too gentle with the pair of killers, pulling them about like hogtied steers, which seeing as they were handcuffed they couldn't do much about. When the doctor had finished his ministrations Quigley asked him about the wounded cowboy.

'None too good. I have him up at my place with Winnie caring for him.'

'Maybe I should mosey up there and have a word with him. If he's fit to talk, that is. I need to find out how the row started. But then maybe Sloane started it deliberately. It was me they wanted. Seems I killed a cousin of theirs, Stonewall Faulks. That was earlier this year. He tried to rob the bank and I guess I put a stop to that. I'm thinking the plan was to lure me down there and bushwhack me.'

'Yeah, I remember the attempt on the bank all right. I guess you saved the state a hanging, seeing as Faulks killed Gale Riley the teller. Made his wife Rhonda into a widow. I don't reckon she's over that yet. Comes regular to me for sleeping draughts.' Doc shook his head. 'Hell of a thing. Hell of a thing. Young fella like that being cut down in the prime of life.'

'Faulks was a mean son of a bitch, all right. One killing I don't regret. But then maybe it would have been better if he had been hanged. Perhaps Sloane and Golay mightn't have come after me then, and that poor cowboy would be back on the trail punching cows.'

'Hell, you don't know how things will work out. You do your damndest and sometime it sneaks up behind you and bites you right on the ass.'

Doc packed his bag and made ready to leave.

'I'll walk back with you, Doc. Look in on that cowpoke and try to find out if he has folks as he might want me to get in touch with.'

3

Quigley stood inside the sickroom looking at the wounded man in the bed. Winnie Reardon, a well upholstered matron, fussed over the young cowboy. Quigley thought the man would have been a good-looking fella when in full health. Right now his face was pale and drawn. Quigley cursed inwardly, thinking the unfortunate man had been but a pawn in the deadly game of death Sloane and Golay had been playing.

'He got any papers on him?' he asked.

'I locked them in the bureau in the front room,' Winnie told him. 'I just know he had a lot of cash on him. I didn't examine anything else.'

'When you're ready I'll have a look.'

She took him through to the front and unlocked the large bureau and showed him the money belt and papers. Quigley counted seven hundred and fifty dollars. Not a fortune, but wealth enough for a cowboy. Browsing through the documents he discovered the money was from the sale of cattle in the name of Peter Barker. He told Mrs Reardon to lock it all away again and went back to the

14

sickroom. He parked himself in a chair and sat watching the man.

'Mr Barker,' he said at last, 'I sure am sorry you got involved in a private vendetta. Those galoots were after me and they used you as a lure to reel me in. I sure as hell hope you survive this.'

To Quigley's surprise the man's eyes opened. He stared blankly around him finally settling on the lawman.

'Howdy,' he whispered. 'Where am I?'

'You're in safe hands, Mr Barker. I'll fetch the doc.'

'That man, he shot me. I never seen him before in my life.'

The words were whispered and weak, and it obviously took him a great effort to speak.

'Doc,' Quigley called.

Mrs Reardon arrived.

'What is it?'

'It's Mr Barker. He's awake.'

Mrs Reardon took a cup and offered it up to the sick man. He sucked weakly at the liquid. While she was doing so her husband came in.

'Ah, I see you are awake, young man,' he said breezily.

'Thank you for looking after me. I must get word to my family.'

Every word was wheezed out with pauses as the man fought for breath.

'Yeah, we'll see to that.'

'I had money. What happened to it?'

'Winnie has your stuff locked away safe. It's all there when you want it.'

There was silence after that. Barker lay with his eyes closed, his breathing shallow. Quigley was about to leave when the man spoke again.

'I ain't going to make it.'

15

'What makes you think that, fella? We'll have you patched up and back on your horse afore too long.'

Again there was a long silence as if the man was mustering his strength in order to speak again.

'Would you write a letter?'

The three people in the room glanced at each other.

'I'll fetch paper,' Mrs Reardon said and left the room.

The two men stood in silence until she returned. She handed the writing pad to Quigley. He looked quizzically at her.

'You're the state's representative, Joshua,' Doc said. 'It's your responsibility.'

It was a long and laborious process involving many pauses as the man told Quigley what to write. In it he told his wife to sell up the ranch and take the money from the sale of the cattle and make a new life for her and their daughter.

'Tell her I love her and sorry I let her down.'

'Mr Barker, you didn't let no one down. You were the victim of a couple of no account killers.'

'I sold my cattle in Templeton. I should have headed for home. Instead I decided to stop off in Idlereach for a bit of fun. Bad call. Maybe my family's better off without me.'

'Peter, don't say that. We all make mistakes.'

'Doesn't matter now.' And then he said something Quigley didn't understand. 'McRae will get what he wants now.'

There was silence, and Quigley, thinking he was finished, folded the paper.

'Mister, will you promise the letter and the money will be delivered?'

'Sure thing, Peter. The mail coach is due through here tomorrow. I'll make sure it's all sent off.'

Peter Barker's eyes fixed on Quigley. 'No, I want you to do it.'

'Yeah, of course; I said I would.'

'Not the mail coach. You deliver it! Promise me. Tell my wife it weren't my fault. Tell her I'm sorry. Promise me.'

For long moments Quigley stared into the dying man's eyes.

'Yeah, I'll do it,' he said reluctantly.

With a deep sigh Peter Barker closed his eyes for the last time. Quigley sat there numb, staring at the grey, lifeless face. A deep anger welled up inside him. Anger at the fate of the dead man. Anger that he was indirectly the cause of an innocent man's death. Anger at the useless slaughter of a good man.

'I guess he's gone,' Doc Reardon said.

Quigley stood up, the letter clutched in his hand.

'He leaves a wife and family behind him and a ranch,' he said, the anger riding him and putting tension in his voice. 'A good man working to provide a life and a future for his family. The scum that murdered him leave nothing behind, only death and misery.'

He fell silent then, the anger burning out to leave a feeling of melancholy.

'God have mercy on his soul,' Winnie said.

'Amen,' Doc added. 'You going to do it, Quigley?'

'Huh!' Quigley looked up.

'You don't have to, you know. Deliver the letter.'

'Heck, Doc, I made a promise.'

Doc nodded his head.

'I'll take care of the burial. We can give him a decent send-off. Use some of that money he had on him.'

'Sure thing, Doc.' Quigley handed over the letter. 'Put that with his things.'

4

Noreen saw the horse and rider out on the flats. She stood in the yard shading her eyes, peering out from the yard. A lone rider was unusual. As a rule they came in a gang. There was a movement behind her and someone came out on the porch. Noreen turned and her mother was there also, squinting under her hand at the hazy figure crawling slowly towards them. It did not need to be asked where he was heading. There was nothing out here but the ranch, surrounded by sagebrush with the occasional stunted oak.

'Who do you think it is?' her mother asked. 'You think Peter's finally come home?'

'Can't tell at this distance. He sure is well overdue.'

Peter Baker had ridden out more than a month ago with a herd of cattle he intended selling in Templeton. Noreen wasn't unduly worried. The trip to the railhead was seventy miles or more, and driving a herd of cattle, no matter what size, was a slow process. Peter had to find a buyer and hammer out a deal. He would then have to wait until his money was secure. Then he still had the responsibility of making sure the cattle were safely loaded on a train that would take them east to the slaughterhouses and city markets.

'Shall I bring the rifle?' her mother asked.

Noreen turned and looked at her.

'It might be someone from the Circle M?' the older

woman said.

'Maybe. You stay inside with it just in case. I'll see what they want first.'

The youngest member of the family came around the corner of the house. She had a bundle of sticks clasped firmly against her body, her little arms barely able to enclose them.

'Jemima,' Noreen said, 'what on earth are you doing with those?'

'I'm building a tepee,' her daughter announced proudly. 'Will you help me?'

'Sure I will. Have you thought where you want to build it?'

'In the vegetable patch. Then Mercy won't eat it.'

'You think mules are partial to tepees?'

'I don't know. I just don't wanna take the chance.'

'How many times have I told you not to say "wanna". Say, "I want to", which is polite and ladylike.'

'Oh, heck ma, that's how Jimmy Sager talks. And his pa owns the Red Nugget saloon and is really rich.'

Noreen looked sharply at her daughter.

'Also young lady, that particular h-word is forbidden in this house.'

Jessica smiled sweetly at her mother.

'Pa says it. I heard him say, "What the heck is that old witch up to now?" '

'I'm sure your father would say no such thing.'

When next she spoke Jessica leaned towards her mother and spoke in a confidential manner.

'I think he was talking about Grandma.'

Noreen couldn't help but glance towards the house.

'Hush child, or I'll be making you wash out your mouth with soap,' she chided. 'Go and put your sticks in the garden. There's a rider coming this way.' She didn't voice her hope that it might be her husband. 'Soon as I see what he wants we'll build you a tepee.'

The girl dropped her burden where she stood.

'Pa is coming,' she squealed and ran to the well where she clambered up on the wall and stood looking out. 'It's Pa!' she yelled and waved frantically. 'Pa!'

'Oh, heck,' Noreen muttered under her breath – and then in a louder voice, 'Careful you don't fall in the well!'

The three females waited in differing stages of anticipation: Jemima in a state of unmitigated excitement, straining on tiptoes to see the rider; Noreen the wife, filled with pleasurable expectation, waiting patiently in the yard; Betsy the grandmother, inside the house, nervously cradling a Winchester rifle, watching the rider coming across the flats and hoping it was the man of the house.

The man riding towards the ranch could see the figure standing in the yard. There was a child standing on something and waving. He didn't wave back – he wasn't the sort of man to make idle gestures. As always, he scanned the horizon on the lookout for other riders, but he could see there was nothing to distract him from his mission with the people at the ranch. He took no pleasure in the task that lay ahead, slowing the pace of the horse the nearer he got.

The woman and child stood in the yard watching as he stepped down from his horse and tied it to the fence before opening the gate and walking up the path. Noreen studied him and noted the twin holsters. Her worst suspicions were confirmed. A gunfighter. The man wore a wide-brimmed black hat which he doffed as he approached.

'Howdy, ma'am. I'm looking for Mrs Barker.'

'Go in the house, Jemima,' she said.

Reluctantly, and keeping a curious eye on the newcomer, Jemima walked backwards to the house. All the while the man kept silent, standing there in the hot sun, holding his hat. Noreen waited until she heard the door before speaking.

'You work for Huston McRae. So let me tell you afore you get those guns out, there's a couple of rifles aimed right at you.'

'Thank you ma'am, I noticed only one rifle. The second one must be very skilled at concealment.'

She blinked some before replying. 'Tell McRae the answer is still the same. We're not selling.'

She stiffened as he slipped a hand inside his vest thinking he had a shoulder holster. When his hand appeared again he was holding a crumpled envelope.

'I have a letter for Mrs Noreen Barker?'

'I'm Noreen Barker. What is that – a writ or something? Tell McRae he's wasting his time. No sale.'

'Just take the letter, ma'am. It might go some way to tell you why I am here.'

Reluctantly she reached out and took the paper. The envelope wasn't sealed. She opened the single sheet of paper. When she glanced at the man, he had turned sideways and was looking into the distance. She began to read. He heard her gasp out loud, and he turned his head towards her.

'What does this mean?' she asked in a low voice.

'It means, ma'am, your husband ain't coming back.'

She was staring straight at him, and it grieved him to see the pain and bewilderment in her eyes. She put her hands to her mouth and her body swayed. For a moment he thought she was about to faint. But she stayed upright, her eyes pools of hurt and bewilderment.

Feeling helpless he mumbled, 'I'm sorry.'

She turned away from him and walked towards the house.

'I got his things,' he said.

She stopped, her shoulders hunched over, then turned back to him.

'I'm sorry, where are my manners? Would you step inside the house?'

'Thank you, ma'am. I'll need to take care of my horse.'

'The corral is that way.' She pointed towards the side of the house. 'You'll find feed in the barn, and water.'

He nodded, placed his hat on his head and walked back to the gate where he had tethered the big roan. When he had the horse rubbed down and had given it plenty of hay and water, he went up to the house, knocked on the door, and then stood back with his hat clasped in one hand and his saddlebags draped over his arm. The door opened and the young woman nodded to him.

'Please come in. We have coffee on.'

5

The room was neat and orderly with basic-looking furniture, some of it plainly homemade. A handsome older woman with auburn hair, streaked with grey, eyed him warily as he stepped inside. The little girl was holding the older woman's hand and staring at the newcomer with wide scared eyes.

'What's your name?'

'Quigley, ma'am.'

He stood ill at ease and wishing he was back in Idlereach – anywhere but here in this house of women.

'Please take a seat.' She guided him to a chair at the

table and poured coffee for him. 'Would you like some-thing to eat?'

To his mortification his stomach growled as if her words had provoked a reaction. The little girl giggled. Quigley reddened and stared down at the deal table.

'Jemima, why don't you take Grandma outside and she can help you put up your tepee.'

The girl was still giggling as the older woman ushered her from the room.

'I'll put the pan on and fry some fatback.'

'Really, ma'am, there's no need to bother.'

'While I cook you can tell me what happened to my husband.'

As she spoke he heard the break in her voice.

'Gee, ma'am, I hardly know where to start.'

The smell of cooking fat filled his nostrils, and his stomach grumbled some more. Hastily he massaged his abdomen.

'Your husband Mr Barker, ma'am, stopped off in Idlereach on his way back from the railhead at Templeton, where he had sold his cattle. I guess he thought he deserved a drink afore heading home. Sadly he got caught up in the crossfire when a couple of gunmen had a shootout. Like I said, I got his belongings in here.' He opened the saddlebags. 'There's money and his watch and things. He asked me to . . .'

The sound of weeping stopped him. He looked up, and she was standing by the window, the pan forgotten, shoul-ders hunched over. Quickly he stood and went to the stove. He heard her sniffling as she tried to stem her grief. Quigley felt awkward and useless. Aimlessly he tended the fatback, not knowing what to say. He sensed her come back again.

'I got eggs,' she said, her voice thickened by emotion.

She took the skillet from him. 'Please sit down.'

He did as she told him, and presently she placed a heaped plate on the table. Before he began to eat he pushed the saddlebags towards her.

'Everything in there belonged to your husband. There's just over seven hundred dollars. There was a mite more, but it went on funeral . . .'

He stumbled to a halt thinking not to go into too much detail. She placed her hand on the saddle-bags but did not explore further.

'Did he suffer?'

'Not much, ma'am. I don't think he felt much of anything.'

'What about the men as shot him?'

'In jail, ma'am. They were wanted men, anyhow. They'll go to the penitentiary or be hanged. That's up to the judge.'

Slowly she slipped her hand inside the saddlebags and pulled out the contents. The money was in a canvas money belt. There was a watch and notebook and papers and tobacco, along with a pencil and a knife.

'There's a handgun and a Spencer rifle. I got those outside in my blanket roll.'

She looked at him and her eyes were muddied with hurting.

'I'm sorry,' he said, feeling helpless.

She was silent, holding the watch and looking down at it, but he did not think she was seeing it. She was seeing the man that belonged to the watch. The silence stretched on and he didn't know how to break it. He finished eating and she refilled his coffee without being asked. In a gesture he felt strangely moving she pushed the makings towards him.

'You may as well have that. No one here smokes.' Her

voice caught again but she rallied. 'I . . . you'll want paying for your trouble.'

She touched the money belt, but stopped when he held up his hand.

'No, ma'am.'

To distract from the awkwardness of the moment he took the tobacco pouch and rolled a smoke.

'How come you got the task of coming here?'

'Mr Barker asked. I made him a promise.'

She nodded slowly. 'Where will . . . I mean when will. . .? When will you start back?'

She stopped and held up the watch. Then she began to speak sonorously, as if she were addressing the man who once carried the timepiece:

'Tomorrow, and tomorrow, and tomorrow,
Creeps in this petty pace from day to day,
To the last syllable of recorded time;
And all our yesterdays have lighted fools.
The way to dusty death. Out, out, brief candle!
Life's but a walking shadow, a poor player,
That struts and frets his hour upon the stage,
And then is heard no more. It is a tale.
Told by an idiot, full of sound and fury,
Signifying nothing.'

She paused before continuing. 'Have you ever heard of Shakespeare, Mr Quigley?'

'Yes, ma'am. When I was herding cattle he used to cook for us cowboys.'

She shot him a startled glance, and then her lips twitched momentarily and some of the tension leaked out from her.

'Mr Quigley, I do believe you just cracked a joke.'

He inclined his head towards her. 'I imagine a very poor one at that.'

Suddenly her shoulders slumped. 'Thank you, Mr Quigley.'

The door burst open and Jemima bounced inside.

'Mummy, mummy, you got to come and see my teepee. Me and Grandma made it.'

'Grandma and I,' Noreen said absently. 'Jemima, I want you to say hello to Mr Quigley.'

She came shyly towards him and he swivelled in his chair.

'Howdy, Miss Jemima. It's a real pleasure to make your acquaintance.'

'Pleased to meet you, Mr Quigley.' She gave a small curtsy.

'You got any Injuns living in that there teepee?' he asked.

She twisted awkwardly and looked towards her mother. Noreen smiled reassuringly at her.

'It's for my dolls.' Her eyes brightened. 'Would you like to see my teepee, Mr Quigley?'

'Sure thing, miss. I used to live in a teepee.'

Jemima's eyes widened. 'Are you an Injun? You don't look like an Injun. Have you got a tomahawk?'

'Jemima,' Noreen cut in, 'it's rude to ask questions. Mr Quigley is our guest.' She paused as if struck by a thought. 'It is a long ride back. You will maybe want to stay the night.'

'I would rest up my horse for a day if that's no inconvenience.'

'I'll make up the bed in the spare room for you.'

'No need to go to any trouble ma'am. I can sleep in the barn.'

'No, Mr Quigley, you will have one night at least in a

comfortable bed. As you don't want paying for your trouble it is little enough to give you a bed and feed you.'

'And a mighty fine feed it was, too.'

Jemima was hopping from foot to foot. 'Oh, Mum, Mr Quigley says he wants to see the teepee!'

Quigley stood. 'I wouldn't be much of a gentleman if I turned down such a gracious invitation from such a charming young lady!'

6

Quigley thought he was an early riser, but when he got up, Noreen was already up and about. He could see dark circles under her eyes, and he was thinking she hadn't slept much.

'I got coffee on the go,' she told him. 'I'll cook breakfast after I've seen to the animals.'

'Thank you, ma'am, anything I can do to help?'

'You've done enough for us, Mr Quigley. Ma will be up later and we manage between us.'

'If you're sure, ma'am?'

She poured coffee for them both.

'I didn't thank you for being so good with Jemima. I'm afraid I was a little out of sorts.'

'She's a good kid. I enjoyed her company.'

'Have you any children, Mr Quigley?'

'No, ma'am.'

'I take it you're not married, then?'

He shook his head and changed the subject.

'When I rode up you asked me did I work for Huston

McRae. Why was that?'

'It was nothing.'

She didn't admit it was the sight of his guns that had prompted the question. A man wearing side arms and carrying a rifle marked him in her mind as a gunman, just like some of the hands that rode for McRae. She noticed he wasn't wearing the gunbelt now.

'The reason I ask, is, your husband mentioned the name afore he died and I'm curious as to the significance.'

She darted a glance at him. 'What did he say?'

He didn't answer her question but asked one of his own. 'Who is this McRae?'

'He owns the neighbouring ranch, the Circle M. Biggest spread around here.' She abruptly stood before he could ask any more questions. 'I must get those chores done.'

Quigley stood up also. 'I'll see to Oasis.'

Her eyebrows lifted.

'My horse,' he said. 'When I've a lot of riding to do I think of that mare as an oasis. She carries my water and food, and brings me safely home again.'

He followed her outside and walked to the corral while she went to let the hens out of the henhouse. The mare was pleased to see him, and he brushed her down. There were two other ponies there, and two ancient mules, and he made sure there was enough feed and water for them all. Satisfied with his work he rolled a quirly and leaned on the topmost rail, staring out across the empty spaces, thinking over all that had happened in the last week, and wondering, too, if Oasis were rested up enough to make the long ride back home.

Quigley was curious about Huston McRae. Noreen Barker had been reluctant to discuss her neighbour, and he remembered Peter Barker's words well enough.

McRae will get what he wants now.

Was Noreen Barker the prize, or was it her ranch? A woman's voice was calling and he turned towards the sound.

'Breakfast! Come and get it.'

His tummy rumbled, and Quigley remembered the same thing happening yesterday. It had amused Jemima but embarrassed him. He went towards the house.

The breakfast was generous, with fresh bread and eggs and fatback and beans. Jemima kept up a steady stream of questions, which Quigley answered with patient good humour. Her mother tried to quieten her down, but Jemima was irrepressible and Quigley told Noreen not to mind.

'It does me good to mix with younger folk,' he told her. 'Mostly I have only grown-up conversation, so it's refreshing to listen to little girl talk.'

He felt at ease as he sat at the table with his third mug of coffee. Noreen's mother chatted to the girl, taking some of the attention off Quigley.

'What time do you want to set off?' Noreen asked. 'Maybe you'll want to make an early start?'

'Mummy says my daddy is gone to heaven,' Jemima piped up. 'She said you were there with him. Why did he go?'

There was an embarrassed silence for a moment before Quigley spoke.

'Well, your daddy didn't have no choice in the matter. You see, life is in some ways like a card game. When the cards are dealt you just got to play the hand you are given. Sometimes it's a winning hand and you get to go on playing the game. When the cards fall wrong you just know you got to fold and then you have to cash in your chips.'

All three females were staring at him and Quigley looked down at the table trying to think of someway else of telling this child what had happened to her pa. He was thinking maybe he had displeased them the way he had depicted Peter Barker's death.

'I see,' Jemima said solemnly. 'Who deals the cards?'

Quigley looked up, surprised at her question, but forged ahead gamely.

'It was two very bad men. They are in jail now, waiting to be tried by a judge. They'll be punished for dealing your daddy such a poor hand.'

Jemima nodded solemnly. 'Did Daddy say anything about me?'

'He said, "Tell Jemima I love her." He said he was sorry he wouldn't be there for you, and he wants you to take care of Mummy and Grandma for him.'

Her eyes brightened at this. 'I will, I will.'

Feeling guilty he dared at last look up directly at the women and was disconcerted to see both had tears in their eyes. Noreen mouthed thank you. Quigley blinked and became acutely self-conscious.

'Thank you for the breakfast. I don't usually have such quality home cooking. I guess I'd better get ready to hit the trail.'

'Do you have to go?' Jemima surprised him by asking.

'Mr Quigley, you are welcome to stay another day or two if you want.'

He paused before saying 'Another day should see Oasis well rested,' not displeased by the suggestion. 'It was a long ride here, and it would be better to give her some more time to recover afore we start back.'

'Oh, good!' Jemima clapped her hands.

'I should like to earn my keep while I'm here. Is there anything needs doing?'

30

'I have to go out and check on the cattle,' Noreen said. 'Perhaps you can help me with that?'

'Sure thing. How many head have you?'

'We did have a lot, but Peter was selling them off. You see, we couldn't get any help and Peter was culling the herd to a more manageable size. We must be down to about four or five hundred head now.'

'I'll be glad to help out. I'll go and get saddled up and wait for you.'

Quigley left the table and went out to the corral. As he threw the saddle on he spoke to his horse.

'Come on, Oasis. We gotta earn our keep. Can't carry on eating our heads off and not doing something in return.'

He led the horse around to the yard. Noreen was already there and mounted on a sturdy mustang. But as he held the gate for her he heard hoofbeats approaching.

7

There were four riders coming towards them at a lively pace. Quigley thought he heard a muttered 'damn!' from his companion, but dismissed it. Noreen was pretty strict correcting Jemima's language, and he didn't associate her with double standards. The quartet drew rein and dust billowed up with their arrival. Oasis sneezed and took a few steps sideways.

'Whoa, girl.'

Quigley patted the horse's neck. Beside him he saw the woman stiffen and her brow was wrinkled in a frown. He got the impression she was not on friendly terms with the horsemen. Examining them he saw all the signs of gun-hands, holstered side arms and rifle butts jutting up from saddle scabbards.

'Howdy, Mrs Barker. We come to offer our condolences.'

The man who spoke was the youngest member of the gang. He was clean shaven, and Quigley figured he was maybe a year or two shy of twenty. His companions he recognized as typical gun hawks, all older by at least ten years than their young spokesman, mean looking and glowering at Quigley in a decidedly unfriendly manner.

'Now you've performed your duty you can turn around and go back to the Circle M.'

Noreen's voice tight and cold. The youngster grinned and leaned his forearms on his saddle horn.

'I see you got a replacement fella. That was pretty slick work. Makes me think as maybe he was hanging around afore your old man got killed.'

'Get off my ranch!'

There was controlled fury in her voice. The youngster threw his arms wide and tried to look offended.

'That is mighty unfriendly of you, Mrs Barker. I only come by to tell you my pa sends his condolences and wants to know when you want to sell up.'

Her face was pale and she was breathing through pinched nostrils.

'You can tell McRae the Barrel B is not for sale. Now if you gentlemen will be on your way I have a ranch to run.'

The kid's eyes flicked to Quigley who had remained silent during this exchange. Quigley was cussing himself for not having the foresight to bring his weapons with him. But then he was not expecting trouble out here on this remote ranch. Not that he could have stood much chance against four armed men who looked like they were no strangers to gunplay. Still, it might have made them a mite more respectful. And then again, maybe not.

'How you going to run the place with poor old Pete gone, God rest his soul?'

One of the men sniggered, which pleased the kid. He grinned over his shoulder. Then he turned his eyes on Quigley.

'You think to run it with this rannie. Hell, he don't look like he'd know one end of a steer from the other. What's your name, fella?'

Quigley stared steadily back. Saw the hunger in the kid's eyes. Spoiling for a fight. Aching to pull one of the big guns he wore and use it. One of the guns was a Colt Walker. It took a skilled gunfighter to use such a big gun. Quigley was wondering who the hell this kid thought he was, packing such a big gun, and wondered if he had ever used it to shoot at anyone.

'Fella, I asked you a question.'

The kid eased his horse around so he had a head-on view of Quigley. It was then that Quigley knew these men were here for him. Either to frighten him off or give him a beating. They must have people watching the ranch, reporting back. Had seen him arrive, and now he was to be dealt with.

A phrase Mrs Barker had used came to him. We can't get help on the ranch, she had told him. And he reckoned this bunch of bullies were the reason. Without cowhands, Peter Barker had been forced to sell off his cattle, reducing his herd to a manageable level that one man and one woman could handle. The kid put his hand on his gun butt. From the expression on his face Quigley knew the kid was not bluffing. He held his empty hands out from his sides.

33

'I ain't packin',' he said.

For long minutes they stared at each other, and Quigley saw the killing lust in those young old eyes. There was a movement from the side as Mrs Barker edged her horse in between the two men.

'Get out of here,' she hissed. 'I want no trouble. This man brought me the news of Peter's death. He'll be gone tomorrow.'

The kid ignored her. 'You lily-livered excuse for a man, hiding behind a skirt,' he said scornfully. He flicked his head. 'Take him, fellas. Break his legs, break his arms, break his fingers, break anything that'll break.'

They jigged their horses around the woman to get at him. Quigley knew he had to move before they could get their hands on him. Unarmed, he knew he was going to take a beating, but he wouldn't make it easy. His boots were out of his stirrups and he swung around – launching himself across the short space between him and Noreen's horse and using its haunches as a springboard, he cannoned into the kid, taking everyone by surprise.

His head smashed into the kid's face and the kid went over backwards, the lawman's hand scrabbling for the big Walker. His fingers curled around the butt, and as the kid fell away from him the gun came free. Quigley swiped at him with its barrel and caught him across the bridge of the nose. The blood was already gushing from that tender organ after Quigley's head butt.

The kid fell to the dirt, and Quigley jumped so his feet were astride him. The stricken man was yelling and cursing, but his yells turned into a frightened squeal when Quigley jammed the barrel of the Walker in his mouth, breaking a couple of teeth as he did so.

'Tell your dogs to back off or I'll blow you to hell and back,' he yelled. 'Now, or you're a dead cowboy.'

The kid's eyes were wide with fright and he spluttered, with blood bubbling from his nose and mouth. There came a yelp, and Quigley looked up. One of the gunnies had an arm around Noreen's waist and his gun was pressed against the side of her head.

'You let up, fella, or the woman gits it. I'll blow her brains out.'

Quigley stared up at the couple. If Mrs Barker was scared she certainly wasn't showing it.

'Kill him,' she yelled. 'Just pull the trigger. It doesn't matter if they kill me. With Peter gone I have nothing to live for. So go ahead and shoot that piece of trash.'

Quigley looked down at the kid trapped beneath him. The youngster was shaking his head from side to side, his eyes open wide as he stared up at his attacker, begging for mercy. There was a mute terror and appeal in his eyes. Quigley glanced back at the gunman holding Mrs Barker.

'Well, fella,' he called, 'you want to take a chance on surviving this, for as sure as this is Wednesday, if I have to pull the trigger I'm turning my gun on you, next. You heard what Mrs Barker said. It makes no difference to her whether she lives or dies.'

'You want this woman's death on your conscience?' the gunman spat back. 'You have the choice of backing off or forcing me to kill her.'

'You haven't the guts to do it,' Noreen said scornfully.

'The Circle M ranch hands are cowards and dog worms.'

There was such cold distain in Noreen's voice it sent a trickle of tension down Quigley's spine. He almost expected the gunman to be goaded by the scorn in the woman's voice and actually put a bullet in her head, and was tensing himself for the action he knew he would have to swing into.

Quigley knew he couldn't kill the kid lying helplessly under his own gun. He would instead concentrate on trying to take out the man holding Noreen Barker, and wondered if he would be fast enough to hit him before he reacted and carried out his threat. It all depended on the gunman's reactions. Even so, if Quigley did hit him square on, his reflexes might just cause him to pull the trigger, putting a bullet in the woman's head. When a gunshot came he almost did pull the trigger, and the kid he held captive would have died there and then. And then he heard someone yelling.

'I can pick you rannies off one at a time if you don't all back off and hang up your shooting irons, pronto.'

Quigley looked towards the voice, and there was Jemima's grandma with a rifle resting on the top of the gate, aiming it at the little knot of horsemen.

'I got a full load here and I won't stop shooting until all those saddles are empty. In case you don't know who is shooting at you, it's Betsy Gallagher. I won the County Top Gun competition back in '77. I still got a good eye in my head. So make your play. It's your choice – boot hill or back to the Circle M.'

Quigley straightened up. He looked down at the man on the ground.

'Tell them, kid. Back off and we can all walk away from this.'

'Grant,' the kid croaked, 'do as he says.'

The gunnies were stymied, with nowhere to go. There was no other option for them. Slowly the gun was lowered from Noreen's head.

'You put your gun up,' he growled at Quigley.

'Ain't my gun. It belongs to your boss here. You do as that lady says and I'll return the gun.'

Reluctantly the gun was holstered. Noreen pulled her mount away and rode clear. Quigley held up the Colt and he could see the gunmen tense. Deliberately he ejected the shells and tossed the gun to the dirt. As the kid rolled to the side and clambered to his feet Quigley reached out and grabbed the second gun from the youngster's holster. He stepped back, carefully watching the horsemen.

It was a bold move. Their weapons were holstered while Quigley now held a loaded gun in his hand. Quigley figured he now held all the aces. A loaded gun in his hand plus the backup of the lady shooter by the gate.

'I guess you fellas have overstayed your welcome. Get this little packrat back on his horse and hightail it out of here. You were lucky today – no one died.'

They weren't happy but they had no choice. As he mounted, the youngster with the bloodied face turned a look of pure venom on Quigley.

'Someday I'm going to kill you.'

They spurred away. A couple of hundred yards out, the horsemen drew pistols and fired in the air. It was a gesture of pure frustration. Quigley watched them go, then turned to look up at his companion. She jigged her horse close to him holding the reins of his own mount.

'I guess you'll want to leave here sooner than you planned,' she told him, as she handed him the reins.

Quigley frowned up at her. 'Does that mean you're withdrawing your hospitality?'

She stared back at him with grave eyes.

'It means I don't want your death on my conscience.'

Quigley swung up on Oasis. He stared out after the departing gunmen.

'Did you mean that about not having anything to live for?' he asked.

She turned and was looking back at the house.

'I have a daughter and a mother to live for. And this ranch. Peter loved this place. He wanted to build it into a prosperous business where he could hire men to work for him. He had all manner of plans. Now he is dead.' She turned back to him and regarded him gravely. 'That was Virgil McRae you just buffaloed. Huston McRae's son. A mean, spoiled brat. Swaggers around like he owns everything and everybody, which under the protection of his father, he more or less does. You asked me about McRae, so now I'll tell you.

'He owns land you couldn't even ride across in a week. He runs more cattle than you could count in a day. He owns businesses too many to name. Timber mills, mines, stores, saloons. He has so much power he controls who buys and sells cattle in this county. That is why Peter had to go all the way to Templeton to sell. McRae blackballed us. We couldn't buy or sell anywhere here.'

Quigley pulled out the makings and rolled a smoke.

'But why? What's so important about this ranch?'

Before she could answer they were hailed from the house.

'You two going to sit out there and jaw all day?'

Noreen pulled her horse around and trotted towards the speaker.

'Coming, Ma.'

Quigley followed with dozens of question buzzing around in his head. He wasn't sure he was going to have answers anytime soon.

9

'Nice shooting there, Mrs Gallagher,' Quigley said, as he and Noreen approached the gate. 'You certainly put a cactus bristle in those fellas' pants.'

She grinned up at him. 'I lied. I never won no shooting competition. But I figured they weren't to know that.'

Quigley grinned back at her.

'You sounded real convincing. I must remember not to play poker with you.'

'Mr Quigley,' Noreen said, 'I'm so sorry you got mixed up in this.'

'I can't figure it. I'm a stranger here. Surely I ain't no threat to them.'

'I told you this ranch is blackballed. They figure you were a new hand we hired so they sent their bullyboys to chase you off. I suggest you do just that and get your stuff and ride out.'

Quigley drew on his smoke and looked at her through the tobacco haze drifting up between them.

'There is the stink of wrongdoing in all this. It ain't legal to threaten ranch hands and make moves to ruin someone's livelihood. Have you or Peter taken your case to the local law?'

'Humph!' it was the older woman who snorted. 'I'll let you guess who gets to appoint the sheriff.'

Quigley looked sombrely at the women.

'It's like that, is it?'

'Yes, Mr Quigley, it's like that. We go into Slimwater and put our complaint to Sheriff Slater. He listens real polite like and then tells us he will look into it. And then does nothing.'

'Let's go in the house and get your things together,' Noreen suggested. 'You can have a coffee and then be well away just in case they decide to come back with reinforcements.'

Quigley turned in the saddle and stared out into the distance as if searching for riders.

'You mentioned Slimwater – is that the nearest town?' he asked.

'It's about six miles south of here. But I wouldn't go there if I were you. A lot of the Circle M crew hang out in the saloons. If any of them recognize you then they'll for sure carry out that beating they threatened, or even worse.'

'Mrs Barker, I don't like being told what I can do or not do. This range stinks worse than a cesspit. There are laws in this country and no matter your status, or how much wealth you own, you have to abide by those laws. It seems to me this place has been taken over by a nest of outlaws, no worse nor no better than the Sam Bass gang. This McRae might be a big shot but he is still subject to the law. Now I can do as you say and ride out of here. If you want me to do that I guess I'd have to abide by your wishes. And then again it might be better if you were rid of me.'

For long, silent minutes the two stared at each other, the only movement the restless stirring of the horses.

'You saying you're not going to let this lie?' she said at last.

'No ma'am, I ain't. A stink is a stink is a stink, and I can't abide the stink of dishonesty in any form.'

'They'll kill you. They've killed before.'

'Even more reason for going after them. I can't abide killers.'

'Come up the house, you pair,' the older woman said, unlatching the gate. 'We'll have a coffee and try to talk him out of this foolishness.'

Jemima's worried little face peeped out from her bedroom when they arrived back in the house.

'Are those nasty men gone?'

'Yes, honey.'

Noreen gathered her daughter in her arms and Quigley smiled at her in what he hoped was a reassuring manner.

'Your grandma chased them off,' he said. 'The females of this household don't let no galoots mess with them.'

The girl came across to him.

'Will you play with me today, Mr Quigley? You can be a chief and I'll be your squaw.'

'Darling, Mr Quigley is going home today. He has his own family to care for.'

'Have you got a little girl?' Jemima asked him.

'No Jemima, I ain't got no family. There is just me.'

'Mama tells me off for saying "ain't".'

'Jemima, go out and play. Mr Quigley has to go on a trip. He's going home.'

Mrs Gallagher served up coffee. Jemima ignored her mother and came and stood by Quigley. He smiled at her and to his embarrassment she wriggled up on to his knee and leaned her elbows on the table, cupping her chin in her hands. He looked with some apprehension at the women. They were both smiling at his obvious discomfiture.

'I can see you have a way with children, Mr Quigley,' the grandma said.

'I . . . uh, don't know much about kids,' Quigley stammered. He took a swig of coffee to cover his awkwardness.

41

He tried to come back to the issue at hand. 'Ma'am, I understand your concern. My staying here is putting you and your family in danger. I wouldn't want that.'

'Oh, they won't harm any of us,' she told him. 'McRae makes it difficult in other ways. If we try to hire help, you saw what happens. Even going into Slimwater for supplies is difficult. We're ignored for the most part by the store owners, and when we persist they overcharge us or tell us they are out of stock, or make distasteful comments.'

Quigley wanted a smoke to help him think, but couldn't see how he would manage it with Jemima perched on his knee.

'I'll move into Slimwater,' he said. 'I'll get a room there.'

Noreen screwed up her face in a frown. 'You don't understand. You're a marked man. You beat and humiliated McRae's son, Virgil. In so doing you awarded yourself a death sentence.'

Jemima squirmed around on his lap and turned big, soulful eyes on him.

'Is that true?' she asked, mirroring the same frown as her mother's.

'I don't think so, Jemima. There are things called laws which prohibit unlawful killing. We are all subject to those laws, no matter how rich or powerful a person is.'

Jemima nodded wisely and went back to her original position.

'I'll get my things and ride out,' Quigley said.

'Wait, if you are determined to stay, there is no need to go into Slimwater,' Noreen told him. 'You're welcome to that spare room as long as you need it. I can see there is no talking any sense into you.'

'Oh, goodie!' Jemima exclaimed, and clapped her hands.

'Thank you, ma'am. Do you know if there is a telegraph office in Slimwater? I need to let my people know where I am at.'

'I can send the message for you. You go in town and you'll be roughed up or slung in jail or worse.'

'I sure appreciate that Mrs Barker, but I might need to wait for a reply.'

'Are you determined to stick your head in the hornet's nest, Mr Quigley?' Noreen said testily. 'And stop calling me Mrs Barker. The name is Noreen, and Mum here is Betsy.'

Jemima clapped her hands. 'And I'm Jemima, Mr Quigley.'

In spite of the tension in the room suddenly everyone was laughing, with Jemima's giggle the loudest. Pleased with herself, Jemima turned to Quigley.

'What is your name, Mr Quigley?' she asked, still giggling.

'Joshua, but near everyone calls me Quigley.'

10

Overlooking Slimwater was a range of mountains Noreen had told him was called Mammoth Peaks. The heights towered black and massive on the horizon. Quigley allowed his horse to take its time coming into the town.

That Slimwater was a prosperous town there was no doubt. Quigley could see numerous side streets tunnelling into the township. The commercial sector was buzzing with pedestrians, and horses and wagons crisscrossed the thoroughfares. He counted three saloons, a gun shop, dress shop, a bank, a livery and, most important of all, a post office. He also noted the jailhouse. Quigley tied up his horse outside the post office and went inside. He had to wait to be served, but when he was, he handed the clerk the message he had written beforehand.

'That'll be six cents,' the clerk told him.

Quigley paid and said he'd come back in a while for the reply. When he left the building he headed for the gun shop. He paused for a while looking at the weapons on display in the window then went inside. The atmosphere was heavy with the smell of oil and metal.

'I need cartridges.'

He bought five boxes for his six-shooters and another four for his rifle.

'I'll pick them up later. I got a mite more shopping to do.'

Unknown to Quigley, a copy of his message was delivered to a room in the Grand Imperial Hotel. What was of particular interest to the man and woman who examined it was the fact that it was addressed to the deputy sheriff, Idlereach Law Office.

'When the rattler holds the high ground the coney sends its mate underground,' the man in the hotel room read aloud. 'What the hell! Idlereach – that name is familiar. Just who is this fella Quigley sending to the law in Idlereach?'

The woman frowned and shook her head. 'Means nothing to me.' She began leafing through a bunch of folders. 'Ah, here we are. Telegraph message came in last week. Barker shot dead in Idlereach. Assassins in jail.'

The pair studied each other pondering on the significance of this occurrence.

'I don't like the smell of this. Better let Slater know.'

Subsequently Sheriff Slater, accompanied by a quartet of deputies, paid a visit to the post office where he ascertained the stranger would be coming back. The telegraph operator gave a description of Quigley and Slater assigned two of the deputies to stake out the post office. Slater sent the other two deputies to find and shadow their quarry.

Unaware of the interest in his activities or of the illegal violation of his privacy by the telegraph operator, Quigley went about his business. He bought supplies, which he collected in gunny sacks and hung on his saddle. The store was just across the road from the Red Nugget Saloon, and he decided that before his return he would pay it a visit. Having nothing more to do, he went back to the post office where the operator handed him his return message.

This coney is heading for the burrow.

There was something furtive in the man's expression which hadn't been the case on his previous visit, which left Quigley wondering. He loitered a moment as if in deep thought and studied the operator. Under his scrutiny the man fiddled with papers and Quigley noted the tremor in his hands and the paleness of his skin. Something was definitely troubling the fellow. Quigley remembered Noreen telling him how McRae and his associates controlled everything in the surrounding area.

Damn, this fella is leaking more than sweat. Someone is keeping tabs on me and will now know I sent a message to Idlereach.

'What's the penalty for interfering with the mail?' he asked casually.

For a moment he thought the man was about to faint, but he gathered his wits and tried to bluster.

'What . . . what do you mean?' he stammered.

'I need you to send another message. Forget the

burrow. Come direct.'

The trembling had become very obvious as the operator complied. Quigley could see the man was terrified. And this only confirmed his suspicions that his movements were being watched.

Quigley stepped outside the post office and stood for a moment rolling a quirly while keenly watching the street. Sure enough he spotted his stalkers – at least two of them. He wandered down to the gun shop and his purchases were waiting for him in a gunny sack.

'How much do you charge to give my guns a quick check over?' he asked.

'No charge.'

Quigley waited while the gunsmith broke both Colts and tested the action. He squeezed oil on the working parts and cleaned it off again while Quigley waited patiently.

'There you go, sir. They're in pretty good order. You obviously look after your guns.'

'Sometimes they're all that stand between a man and eternity,' Quigley replied laconically, thinking of the men shadowing him.

This was McRae's town, and according to Noreen he owned the law. He gazed speculatively at the gunsmith and wondered if the man also had to report his purchases to the town boss. Quigley picked up his gunnysack, weighing heavy with the ammo, and bidding the man 'good day', left the store.

Again he spotted his shadows and wondered how many altogether were on his tail. They would know how he had buffaloed the men sent out to deal with him at the Barrel B, so this time they would make sure and beef up the ambush crew.

Sauntering along the boardwalk Quigley paused

ostensibly to examine the menu posted outside a restaurant but in reality to check out the men dogging him.

He continued on towards the saloon he had spotted earlier. It wasn't quite noon yet and the place wasn't busy. Quigley ordered a beer and waited. His shadows entered and positioned themselves around the room. Now they were this close Quigley could see law badges and wondered which one was Slater. Another man came in sporting a sheriff's badge and Quigley knew this had to be Slater. The sheriff was dark haired and of muscular build and not quite as tall as Quigley. The lawman came straight over to him.

'What's your name, fella?'

'Name's Quigley. Who are you?'

'I'm Sheriff Slater and I'm arresting you on suspicion of assault and attempted murder.'

Quigley took a sip from his beer.

'That's the damndest thing I've ever heard. I only been in your town about an hour or so. I ain't had time to assault no one.'

'You pulled a gun and pistol whipped a citizen of this town, one Virgil McRae. He filed a complaint against you. I have a warrant for your arrest. Hand over your guns.'

'This McRae fella, he tell you he brought a bunch of bully boys along, with the intention of beating the pith out of me? If I hadn't dissuaded them I'd'a ended up a pulverized mass of festering flesh somewhere out on the prairie.'

Slater frowned. 'Mr Quigley, you'll get your chance to plead your case in court. Now just do as I say, and hand over those irons.'

Quigley knew he must not be taken in by the sheriff. He had known towns just like this one, where a powerful baron ruled the roost. There was every chance he would die in custody or they might just decide to hang him. He held up his tankard.

'Can I finish my beer first?'

At that point Slater pulled his gun and Quigley threw the beer in the lawman's face.

As their boss stumbled back against the bar cussing, his deputies pulled guns and started forwards. Quigley hauled the sheriff to him, effectively using his body as a shield in case the deputies were tempted to start shooting. At the same time he wrenched Slater's gun from his grip and fired a shot into the ceiling. That stopped everyone dead in their tracks. With his back against the bar and shielded by the sheriff, Quigley tried to figure out his next move.

'If you try to rush me I'll kill your boss. I got nothing to lose.'

'Damn you,' Sheriff Slater spluttered, 'you're in real trouble now. Release me afore you get yourself deeper in.'

'What was the plan?' Quigley asked. 'Your boss order you to bring me in on trumped-up charges? Was I to die trying to escape or resist arrest, or were you told to hang me?'

For a moment there was no reply, and Quigley knew he had guessed right.

'Damn your eyes,' the sheriff swore, 'No one tells me who to bring in. I'm the law in this town. I try to keep order and arrest troublemakers, and you sure are one of them. Now let me go. It'll go easier on you in court if you give up peaceable.'

'Yeah, if I ever get to court. You're a disgrace to your badge, Slater. Crooked lawmen give the job a bad name. Put a badge on a black hat and he's still a black hat.'

As he spoke Quigley sensed a movement behind him. He tried to twist about but was too late as the barkeep swung a lead-weighted club and coshed him. Such was the force of the blow he was driven forward, his senses reeling. He struggled to keep his grip on the sheriff, but it was a losing battle.

Slater jerked free and grappled with the stricken man, wrenching his gun back and using it to strike Quigley on the side of the head. It was enough to put Quigley in the sawdust. As he collapsed the sheriff booted him in the face. It was the signal for his deputies to wade in.

They crowded around eager to get in on the action. Boots thudded into the unconscious man on the floor as the lawmen vented their anger on this foolhardy person who had dared to challenge them on their own turf.

11

Noreen let her horse idle its way through the cattle. For the first time in the last couple of days she was alone. That is if you could call it being alone amongst a herd of cattle. She rode through the herd, listening to the familiar sounds of contented animals as they bawled and called to each other. The constant melody of mooing was having a peculiar effect on her feelings. She had often accompanied her husband when he rode out to attend his herd. Now she felt the full effect of his loss. For the sake of her family she had tried to be brave and not give way to her sorrow. But now in the midst of this familiar task, buried emotions were being released. Noreen let go the reins and cupped her face in her hands as the grief welled up.

'Oh Peter,' she whimpered, 'why, why, why?'

The floodgates opened then as the tears flowed, wetting hands and cheeks. There in the midst of the bawling cows she sobbed like an inconsolable infant. Her shoulders heaved as heartache completely overwhelmed her.

'Peter,' she mumbled over and over again.

It was as if the animals sensed her grief. They closed around horse and rider, their mooing softening and becoming melancholy. And somehow it was calming that these beasts understood her mood and were doing their best to comfort her. Through her tears Noreen smiled weakly.

'Thank you,' she said.

Slowly she got herself under control again and continued her rounds. It was later she spotted the riders far out amongst the sage and stopped her horse and observed them. She was suspicious of all horsemen since the Circle M began their campaign of intimidation. She brought up the glasses and focused on the group.

They milled around for some moments. At this distance she could not make out who they were. Whatever it was that had brought them there had concluded. They reined their mounts about and rode away.

Noreen was puzzled. The riders had left a horse behind. She could see it plainly, head bowed. She focused again on the bunch of riders but they kept on going. The odd behaviour puzzled her. Why abandon a horse out in this deserted place? She focused again on the horse and noted it was saddled.

'What on earth,' she muttered.

And then she had an inkling of what was going on. She had an idea the animal was injured in some way. It was being abandoned out here to die. And she was angry. The humane thing would be to shoot the beast rather than let it linger in isolation and suffering. On impulse she jigged her pony forwards, easing her way through the herd. She had her rifle with her and would perform the act of mercy that unnatural crew had failed to do.

The saddled horse heard her coming and raised its head to look. It whickered as it spotted her. A stone dropped into Noreen's stomach. She knew that horse. It had ridden away from the Barrel B that morning.

At first she thought he was dead. There was no movement and blood had congealed in his ear and there were dried streaks in his hair and along the side of his head. Noreen dismounted and tremulously examined him. At last she detected a pulse – weak and thready.

She was undecided what to do. Experimentally she tugged at him but soon realized there was no way she could get him back up on his horse. What to do? She had to get help and the only help was back at the ranch. Noreen tethered Quigley's mount to a sturdy tree before climbing on her own horse and racing back home.

Once she was fixed on the course, Noreen doggedly set about the project. With the help of her mother, she harnessed up the buckboard. Though she was reluctant to involve her daughter, Jemima insisted on accompanying them. All three of them went to the rescue. Arduous and stressful the whole process was, but eventually they got the injured man back to the ranch.

It was then Betsy took over. Her experiences as a nurse during the war stood her in good stead, and she knew exactly what to do. Noreen helped where she could, and eventually the older woman stood back with hands on hips and surveyed her work.

'Well, we've done our best, Noreen. The rest is up to Mr Quigley. It was a pretty bad going-over they give him. Did you see who they were?'

'Nah, it was too far.'

'Whoever did it weren't expecting him to survive. If anyone came across him they might assume he came off his horse. I could smell whiskey on him but none on his breath. Someone soused him so if he was found it would look like he was drunk and fell off his horse and died from his injuries.'

'He left here with the intention of riding to Slimwater. Didn't say what his business was. We both know who runs Slimwater. They couldn't do their dirty work here, so they waited until they got him on their own soil and attacked him there. It's bestial behaviour.' Noreen gestured towards the unconscious man in the bunk. 'What danger is this man to them? He's a complete stranger; comes here on an errand of mercy and they beat him so badly he might not survive.' Noreen shook her head in despair. 'It's bestial, I tell you. It's bestial.'

'Not only is it bestial,' Betsy responded, 'but cowardly. I wonder how many it took to subdue him. I just hope he hurt a few afore they took him down. Well, we can do no more for the poor fella. Just let him sleep and keep him comfortable and hope he wakes up.'

12

Quigley opened his eyes. A face was looking down on him. The face was dark complexioned with a shock of black woolly hair on the top and with matching cluster on the chin. It was a big face as was suitable for the man who owned it. Deputy Murray Fishbourne weighed at least two hundred and fifty pounds and was a few inches above six feet.

'Man, you sure like to sleep,' Murray said.

Quigley closed his eyes.

'Can you talk?'

But Quigley didn't answer – he was trying to get things right in his mind. At last he opened his eyes again.

'How did you get here so soon?'

Murray's brow wrinkled.

'I was three days on the trail. You know my hoss don't like to hurry.'

Quigley thought some on this.

'Three days, how long have I been lying here?'

'Well, you figure it. I got here yesterday.'

Quigley tried to sit up and winced as pain slithered through every portal of his body.

'Hell, damnit,' he muttered and slumped back again. 'They really worked me over.'

'Want to tell me about it?'

'Ain't much to tell,' Quigley said. 'Went into town. The sheriff of Slimwater and his deputies beat the hell out of me. Don't how I got back here.'

There was movement by the door and the two women of the house came inside the room.

'You're awake,' Noreen said. 'Thank God! We thought you were never going to wake.'

'How come I ended up back here?'

'You were dumped out on the range,' Betsy told him. 'Noreen found you. The people who did it didn't expect you to be found so soon. You were meant to die out there.'

'I guess I owe you my life.'

'You owe us nothing,' Noreen told him. 'It was because of us you were hurt. If you had heeded us and gone back home this wouldn't have happened.'

'He always was a stubborn son of an armadillo,' Murray said. 'You can stomp him, beat him, shoot him, and the danged fool will just keep on coming back.'

Jemima was the next to appear. She squeezed in beside Murray.

'Mr Quigley, I've been praying for you,' she told him. 'I asked God to make you better.'

'Thank you, I knew someone must have been looking out for me.'

'You have to eat,' Noreen said. 'I made some beef stew. Do you think you could eat some?'

'I guess, and thank you for looking out for me.'

When Noreen came back she brought a steaming bowl of stew and a few hunks of bread. It was with great difficulty the injured man was able to sit up. Every segment of his body ached. He tried not to groan out loud as the aches in his body threatened to overwhelm him. He took the bowl from Noreen.

'Thank you.'

'Everybody out,' Noreen ordered. 'Let the man eat in peace.'

Every day Quigley made steady progress. A week later he was sitting on the veranda watching Murray and Jemima. The little girl was perched on the big man's shoulders squealing with excitement while he lumbered around making horsey noises. Every now and then he would pretend to stumble and fall causing the youngster to grip tight to his head and squeal even louder. Betsy came out and handed Quigley a mug of coffee. She sat down beside him with her own mug.

'When he rode up to the ranch, we got out the guns. We were sure it was someone sent by McRae to move us on. We were terrified when we saw that big mulatto stride up to the house and wondered whether to shoot or not afore he reached us and beat us to death. Now look at him. That girl has him run ragged.'

'Murray is all hard on the outside and soft as bread dough on the inside,' Quigley told her. 'Where has Noreen gone?'

'She went out to check the herd. She been so busy worrying about you she got to forgetting about the cows.'

'Sorry for causing you all this bother,' Quigley told her. He began rolling a smoke.

'Huh, the bother started with Justin McRae.'

'Justin!' Quigley paused with the lighted Lucifer halfway to his finished quirley. 'I thought his name was Huston.'

'Justin is Huston McRae's younger brother; Virgil's uncle. It all started when he took a shine to Noreen. I don't hold with gossip, but Noreen will never tell you this. Justin took to pestering Noreen every chance he got. It got so bad she couldn't go into town but he waylaid her. She wouldn't tell Peter for fear of what he would do. In the end Peter did find out and they had a fight – Peter and Justin. Peter gave him a thrashing, and that was the start of our troubles.'

'Hell gnaw their bones!' By now Quigley had his smoke fired up. 'What a repellent family! I've only met Virgil and he was a loathsome jackanapes. It seems the other members of the family are equally vile.'

'I never told you any of this.' Betsy said, as she stood up. 'I'd better get that bronco a mug of coffee afore Jemima drives him into the dirt.'

'Aw he's happy as a mongoose,' Quigley told her. 'He ain't much removed from a big kid himself.'

It took all of Betsy's grandmotherly skills to coax Jemima down from Murray's shoulders so as he could sit on the porch and have a coffee. Even then the youngster insisted on perching on the big man's knee. It was this homely scene that greeted Noreen when she rode into the yard, but the little group sensed from the look on her face that something was seriously wrong.

'You're just in time for coffee,' Betsy called.

Her daughter did not answer. She carried on into the corral and tended to the pony. Then she trudged up to the house, her head bowed.

'What is it, honey?' Betsy called. 'What's the matter?'

Noreen raised her stricken face to them.

'The herd – it's gone. Someone's stolen the herd.'

13

Quigley sat his horse staring out across the flatlands. In the distance rose the bulk of Mammoth Heights. That was the direction the rustlers had driven the herd. Quigley turned to Murray.

'They'll take them into the hills and maybe hold them there a few days while they change the brands.'

'Barrel B, how they going to work that?'

'Barrel can be changed to Circle and B easily becomes 8. If they weren't too bothered about being caught they could go for a simple change to Barrel 8.'

'You reckon they'll get away with that?'

Quigley looked out towards the hills. 'Nothing moves around here without the say-so of the McRaes. I'd say those rustlers know they can do what they like around the

Barker ranch. When I arrived here four gunhands rode out to give me a beating. McRae figured I'd come to work for Noreen so his men came to chase me off. When that didn't work they got me in town instead.'

'That was some beating you took. According to the women when they found you they weren't sure if you were alive or dead.'

'I owe them women. I would have been dead but for them.'

'Are you sure you're up to this?'

'I guess I've been in better shape. Right now I could do with another week of sitting out on that porch while those females fuss over me.'

'They're good people, all right,' Murray opined. 'They don't deserve all this hassle. Sure was bad luck Mr Barker getting himself killed.'

'That weren't bad luck. That was a coldblooded, pre-meditated murder.'

Murray turned in his saddle and frowned over at his companion.

'What you saying, chief?'

'I figure that murder was ordered from right here.'

'The hell you say!'

Quigley told his deputy about his suspicions regarding the telegraph office and the fact that messages in and out of Slimwater were being monitored.

'I reckon someone followed Peter Barker and paid Todd Sloane and Blane Goley to kill him. It was a clever plan to murder him so far from home. Then no suspicion would be laid at McRae's door.

'Once the people here knew I had telegraphed Idlereach, they put two and two together and figured I was too close to the truth. It was too risky to let me live. They tried to make it look like an accident. They think they're clever, these people – covering their tracks to keep suspicion away from the coyote that controls it all.'

'Huston McRae!'

'Yeah, Mr Huston McRae.' Quigley's voice was cold with a touch of flint. 'He is a malevolent tyrant squatting over this community, weaving threads of fear and deceit and criminal cover-ups. He has power and wealth and thinks it gives him licence to ride roughshod over the laws of this country. McRae has created a rats' nest where he is the Lord of Misrule. Twice he tried to have me killed. And that makes it kind of personal.'

'OK, chief; let's make tracks after those rustlers. Try and get Mizz Barker's cattle back.'

They rode all that day. The sun was dipping below the horizon throwing long shadows across the earth without them catching any sight of the rustled herd when they pulled up for a confab.

'Should we carry on and risk stumbling into a gopher hole in the darkness, or haul up and camp for the night?' Murray asked.

Quigley squinted at the night sky. He was bone weary, and would have liked nothing better than to fall from his horse and crawl into his bedroll.

'I guess we should bunk down for now. We should catch up with those rustlers sometime tomorrow.'

He was casting his eye around for a suitable place to set up camp when the shot blasted out of the gloom. Swiftly he slid from his horse. As he hit the ground he could see his pardner's horse down on its knees. It whinnied as it struggled to stand – the sound of an animal in pain. Quigley guessed the horse had been hit. It suddenly nose-dived into the dirt, snorting and grunting, and he realized it had received a serious wound. More shots winged their way.

'Murray, are you hit?'

'No, he got the horse. Damn animal must have sensed someone out there and threw up its head. Took the bullet that was meant for me.'

There came the crash of a handgun as Murray put the wounded animal out of its misery. Quigley flinched with the shot. The horse ceased moving and stopped making those ghastly grunting noises.

'You see where that bushwhacker is firing from?' Murray called.

'About twenty degrees to the right of the setting sun,' Quigley answered. 'Let's go get him.'

'Too goddamn right we will.'

'Fire a few shots at him while I circle around and sneak up on him. If only one of us is shooting he might figure he got the other one with that first shot.'

Murray's answer was to start firing, placing shots in and around the area Quigley had indicated. He got a reply with a flurry of shots from the ambusher, so Quigley was able to home in more accurately on the shooter's position. He moved out, hoping the poor light would mask his movements.

The ambusher was in a dense growth of sage. Bending low, Quigley stalked forwards. He still felt aching and stiff from the beating he had taken from the boots and pistol butts of Sheriff Slater and his deputies. But there was anger there as well, and that drove him on, overriding any discomfort he might feel. The man out there with the rifle had shot to kill, and only by odd chance was it Murray's mount that had been hit and not the man himself.

There was a regular gun battle going on between Murray and the bushwhacker – the louder crack of the rifle distinct from Murray's revolver shots. Briefly Quigley wondered why Murray wasn't using his long gun.

Whatever the reason, he was hoping that because only one gun was firing back at him the rifleman might believe he had put down one of the riders and was now concentrating on taking out the other. That being the case he might not be expecting an attacker sneaking up on him. Almost on cue he heard Murray yelling at the gunman.

'Damn you, you've killed my partner. You ain't leaving here alive.'

By now Quigley had flanked the rifleman, and holding his Colt in front of him, worked his way steadily towards the rifle flashes.

'I got you pinned down,' came the reply. 'Once my pals hear the gunshots they'll come running. Say your prayers, fella. This is the end of the road for you.'

Quigley had no way of knowing if the man was bluffing. Either way he had to be taken down. If his pals arrived, as he claimed they would, his and Murray's chances of getting out of the ambush were an awful lot slimmer.

'You stole my cattle,' Murray called. 'I ain't letting up till I get them back.'

'It's your choice, fella. You'll not have no use for cattle in boot hill.'

And then Quigley could see him – a dim outline behind the rifle he was using. He drew a bead on the shape.

'Fella,' he called, 'if you want to go on living, throw down that rifle.'

Quigley had a feeling the man wasn't going to surrender so easy. And he was right. The rifle swung towards him and a bullet blasted in his direction. Quigley had his Colt centred on the man's chest and he pumped two bullets into the target. There came a coughing sound and the man disappeared into the undergrowth. Quigley waited, but no more sound came from the stricken man.

Murray had stopped firing, probably thinking he didn't

want to shoot his partner by accident. Quigley slowly stepped forward, his weapon at the ready, trying to make as little noise as possible – carefully parting the straggly branches of sage, watching for signs of the ambusher suddenly coming to life again. They were fraught moments as he crept forward.

'You all right?' Murray called. 'What's happening?'

Quigley could not reply for fear it would alert his victim. He heard a low moan and went even more cautiously. At last he could make out a dark form on the ground.

'You make a wrong move, fella, and I'll put another one in you,' he called.

There was no response. Quigley came closer and prodded the ambusher with his boot. The stricken man moaned.

'You can come on up now, Murray,' Quigley shouted. 'I've drawn this snake's fangs.'

14

Together the lawmen squatted by the downed ambusher. They had removed his guns – a holstered Walker Colt and a lever-action Henry rifle, which was the gun he had been using to fire on them. The man was barely alive. He groaned and opened his eyes.

'Son of a bitch,' he wheezed. 'I reckon you've done for me.'

'No more than you were trying to do to us,' Murray told

him. 'Who you working for?'

'Go to hell! Just finish me. I ain't tellin' you nothing.'

'Can you hear that?' Quigley said lifting his head as if listening to something. 'That's a coyote calling, if I'm not mistaken. I guess that old coyote will bring his family down here for a good old feast. The smell of blood will get their juices flowing. We'll leave you to it, fella. Happy feasting.' He stood. 'Come on, Murray. The sooner we're away, the sooner those coyote teeth can be tearing lumps of this fella's face.'

'They like the innards best,' Murray said. 'I saw them coyotes rip a fella open in the twinkling of an eye. Pulled his guts out and were chewing away while they were still attached. Man, I can still hear that fella squealing. Gave me nightmares for days after.'

'Let's get the hell away from here,' Quigley said. 'I don't think I want to see or listen to that. I feel bad just hearing you say it.'

'Wait, wait!' the dying man gasped. 'Finish me off. Don't let those critters get to me.'

'You tell us what we want to know, and we might just take pity on you.'

'We work for the Circle M. Were told if we took the herd we could sell it and keep the money. I was to watch our back trail in case we were followed. We heard there were a couple of fellas working at the Barrel B.'

'Who gave the orders?'

'Hagerman.'

'Hagerman!' Quigley repeated.

'Yeah, he's ramrod at the Circle M. Now finish me like you said.'

'Stanley Hagerman?' Quigley asked. There was no reply. Quigley shook the man. 'Is his full name Stanley Hagerman?'

'Hold it,' Murray said. 'I think he's gone.'

'I got to know if it's the Hagerman I'm thinking of.'

'You know this Hagerman?'

'Not personally, but I know of his reputation. Rumour has it he took over the Hamilton Corcoran gang when Corcoran was killed by Texas Rangers. It was claimed, as an act of revenge, he attacked and laid waste to the town of Wildbluff, the home town of Chester Newell, the Texas Ranger who led the posse. The gang slaughtered men, women and children, and burned the town.' Quigley paused and stared into the dusk before continuing. 'He went to ground after that. If this Hagerman is the same one, then we got big trouble on our hands. He is just the sort of snake who would know how to contact Todd Sloane for the job of killing Peter Barker. And I guess maybe some of the old Corcoran gang is with him. All hardened killers.'

'Maybe coming here was a mistake,' Murray said.

'You think so?'

'There is a way that seemeth right unto a man, but the end thereof are the ways of death.'

In spite of himself Quigley smiled. 'You got a verse of the Bible for whatever terrain you happen to find yourself in.'

'I know you are not a believer, Quigley. But all life is in the Good Book. It is God who equips me with strength and makes my way blameless. He makes my feet like the feet of a deer and sets me secure on the heights. He trains my hands for war so that my arms can bend a bow of bronze.'

Quigley climbed stiffly to is feet, his body feeling the aches and pains of the recent beating he had taken.

'I guess it's pointless blundering on any further with darkness coming down. We'd best move away from here in case those rustlers come to investigate the shooting.

They'll sure be edgy when their pal doesn't show up. I'm reckoning they can't be that far ahead of us.'

'Yeah, our dead friend here did say they would come. We'll find a place to bed down for the night. Set a watch.'

'See if we can find his horse. You'll need a mount now yours is down.'

The horse was hobbled a couple of hundred yards back from the site of the ambush.

'You'll have to help me get my stuff. Damn horse rolled over on top of my saddle scabbard. Couldn't get at my rifle.'

Between them they transferred Murray's saddle and belongings to the new mount, then found a place to make camp well away from the dead rustler. They lit no fire and made do with beans and biscuits washed down with water.

'Sure could do with a mug of Arbuckle,' Quigley said as they ate their meagre supper.

'You and me both. We'll have to take turns standing watch. Don't want no more nasty surprises while we're asleep.'

During the night they were disturbed by the racket from what sounded like a pack of wild dogs fighting over something and surmised the dead rustler was providing the animals with a late supper. Other than that the night passed uneventfully. In the morning they risked a small fire to brew up, and drank hot coffee along with beans and biscuits.

It was easy to pick up the trail of the stolen cattle, and the pair resumed their pursuit. They surmised the rustlers would be aware that someone was trailing them when their rear guard didn't show up. With this in mind they kept a lookout for another ambush. Mid-morning they came upon a deserted campsite and evidence of disturbed scrub where the rustlers had held the herd.

'They ain't far ahead now,' Murray observed. 'We should catch up sometime today.'

'How far ahead you think they are?'

'No more than a few hours.'

Quigley sat his horse staring into the distance. Murray glanced sideways at him.

'What you figuring?'

'I'm thinking we could swing around and get ahead of them. When they bunk down tonight we could maybe spook the herd and start it running back towards their home range again.'

A frown formed on Murray's face. 'God's lid, that could be a mite risky in the dark.'

'You got a better idea? The alternative is a shootout in broad daylight.' Quigley shrugged. 'Hell, we don't know how many they are. There could be anything up to half a dozen or more riding that herd.'

'Yeah, maybe you're right. We ain't got nothing to lose excepting our lives.'

15

The two men rode hard, striking out at an angle from the direction they estimated the herd was taking. During the ride they saw no sign of their quarry. After some hours of riding they began to cut across towards the angle of travel they estimated the rustlers were taking.

Both men were weary when towards nightfall they saw

the herd in the distance. They went cautiously, riding parallel to the herd for fear of being spotted, keeping their distance. Using glasses they were able to monitor the movements of the cowboys tending the cattle. As dusk gathered they found it harder to spot the riders in the poor light so they ventured closer.

'We got to let them settle for the night,' Murray said. 'They'll have some stand guard on the herd while the others roll up in their blankets.'

'I can't see them needing many on night guard,' Quigley observed. 'Doubtless them cows will be leg weary after all this travelling. They'll maybe have only one rider on the lookout for wolves or coyotes.'

Not long after that, the herd came to a standstill and the watchers waited to see a campfire flare into life.

'Hell, I could do with a mug of Arbuckle,' Murray grumbled.

'We need to let them get well settled afore we make our move. Maybe we should get some shuteye while we wait. Take turns watching in case we oversleep.'

They bedded down in a cluster of chaparral and ate a cold supper of beans and jerky washed down with water from their canteens.

'I could murder for a hot steak right now,' Murray mused. 'Washed down with a cold beer.'

'Yeah, well there's plenty of steaks just across from us. Why don't you mosey over and cut us both one. I'll get the fire going and we can cook them afore we make our move against those rustlers'

'Nah.' Murray shook his head. 'We ain't got no onions to go with it, nor potatoes. Wouldn't be the same without the trimmings.'

'I guess you're right at that. Tell you what: as soon as we've done with this business I'll take you to a steakhouse and treat you.'

'I'll hold you to that, Quigley.'

Murray volunteered to take first watch. Quigley lay on his back gazing up at the stars, thinking how peaceful the world seemed. In the distance he could hear the mellow sounds of the herd as it settled for the night. He reflected on the set of circumstances that had brought him here – skulking in the brush awaiting a confrontation with a bunch of killers. In other times he had lain like this in the night, the sounds and smells of the cattle familiar as breathing – and not for the first time wondered if he would have been better to have stayed a cowpuncher.

But because of his skills with the gun he had ended up with a badge and the job of keeping the peace. And now he had been drawn into a confrontation with a violent gang of criminals. Added to that he was in unfamiliar territory, unable to tell friend from foe. And as far as he could make out there weren't many, if any, friends, anywhere near. McRae had everything sewn up tight, and Quigley guessed that those who went against him ended up dead like Peter Barker, or driven out.

He wondered what Huston McRae looked like, and about the McRae family in general. He had already met Virgil – a vicious brat. If the rest of the family were cast in the same mould then he was dealing with a dangerous and ruthless crew with no respect for the law. In fact they owned the law, such as it was in Gila County. This led his thoughts to the Barker family, hewn down to a trio of females, now that the man of the family was dead.

He remembered the way Noreen had reacted during the encounter with Virgil McRae and his bullies. He reckoned most women and a lot of men would have collapsed or fainted when faced with such a threat. With a gun at her head she had not buckled.

A backbone of steel was how he would have described her. She had defied the gunman to do his worst. She had yelled at him to shoot Virgil McRae, surprising even him. Quigley's lips twitched when he recalled that moment. The terrified look in the youngster's eyes when Noreen told Quigley to shoot. It had all been a wonderful bluff, and he wondered what would have happened if Betsy had not intervened.

'Women of steel,' he muttered, not realizing he had spoken out loud.

'What you say?' Murray called.

'Did them females tell you what happened at the ranch the day after I arrived?'

'Nope, only told me how they found you half dead lying out in the chaparral.'

So Quigley told him how the bullyboys had come out to brace him and been sent off with their tails between their legs by the actions of the two resolute women.

'That Betsy, she sure one fine-looking woman,' Murray remarked when Quigley finished his tale.

'Yeah, they both are. Damn shame about Peter Barker. He had everything to live for. That rare family waiting for him back home, and he gets rubbed out because of a grudge held by a man who considers he's above the law.'

Quigley lay back again and Murray went back to keeping an eye on the activity, or lack of it, at the rustlers' camp. The next thing Quigley knew was Murray gently shaking him awake.

'What is it?'

'Time for us to make a move. It must be well past midnight.'

'What! I thought we were to share the watch.'

'You looked so peaceful lying there I hadn't the heart to disturb you.'

'Murray, I don't need mollycoddling. I can hold up my end.'

'Hell, ya just crawled out from a sickbed. I figured you looked so peaceful I hadn't the heart to disturb you.'

Mumbling something about not being an invalid, Quigley came to his feet.

'You got a plan, boss?'

Quigley gave a huge stretch with his arms above his head before replying.

'Unroll your slicker afore we go over there.'

'My slicker! I don't see no sign of no rain.'

'Just do it. All will be revealed.'

The night seemed hushed. Even the cattle were quiet. But Quigley was about to liven things up a mite.

16

As they rode closer to the herd there was no sign of a night guard. The plan was for Murray to stay on the nearside of the cattle while Quigley rode across in the opposite direction.

'When I get into position I'll start the circus. As soon as you hear the commotion you go also. Remember, just ride with the herd once it starts to run. Don't stop for nothing.'

'Got it. We stay with the herd and meet up along the way.'

'Good luck!'

'God go with you,' Murray said.

Quigley rode wide of the dozing animals, not wanting

to get them restless and spooked before he was in position. The smells and sounds of the nearby cattle played on
the senses of the man riding through the night intent on
disrupting the peacefulness of the herd.

Above him stars sparkled in the soft velvet of the sky.
The sage had taken on a murky purple glow. The serenity
of the night and the familiar sounds of the nearby herd
lulled Quigley into a brooding remorsefulness when he
contemplated what he was about to do.

He, along with his deputy Murray, would stampede the
herd, and in the confusion and noise they would follow on
its tail. Quigley was aware that the rustlers' camp was in
danger of being overrun and that bothered him. He tried
to shrug the thought away.

'Hell, they made their choice when they stole the
cattle,' he muttered. 'Where I come from they hang stock
thieves.'

He caught movement ahead of him and blinked in surprise. A horseman was coming towards him. Somehow
Murray, during his night vigil, had missed seeing this one
lone night-rider.

Quigley kept going, wondering how to handle this. He
tugged the brim of his hat down low and hoped in the dim
light the man might mistake him for a member of the
gang.

'What time is it?' the oncoming rider called out. 'That
shift passed a mite quickly.'

Quigley called out something incoherent. And all the
time they were approaching each other. And then the
rustler sensed something amiss.

'Doggone, you're that cowpoke from the Barrel B.'

As he recognized Quigley the rider went for his
weapon. Quigley kneed his horse forwards, at the same
time swiping at the man with his slicker. Instinctively the

man jerked on this reins, not aware it was only a rain cape. As they drew alongside Quigley threw himself at the rustler, crashing into him and unseating him. They both went down, Quigley feeling the pain in his bruised body as they hit the dirt.

Fortunately the slicker hampered his opponent's movements and Quigley smashed his fist into the man's face as he was struggling to get his weapon free. Again and again he hammered at the man, hoping he was doing enough to silence him. The rustler was cursing and threshing about, with Quigley on top pounding at him. Then an arm came up out from under the slicker with a gun gripped in the fist. Too late Quigley saw the gun and then it cracked against his skull and lights exploded in his head.

Blindly he reached out and grabbed for the gun. His hand closed over the man's wrist. The rustler was straining to line up the weapon. Then came the sound of hoofs fast approaching and a horseman loomed up beside them. Quigley saw something coming at them and threw himself aside. The man on the ground grunted as a rifle cracked into his head. Quigley looked up to see Murray looking down at him from the back of his horse.

'Make sure he's out of it,' Murray hissed.

Quigley grabbed the gun from the slack hand of the rustler and used it to club him again.

'I guess you picked the short straw tonight, fella,' Quigley told the unconscious man as he struggled to his feet. 'Thanks, Murray.'

'Where did he come from?'

'Hell knows, just appeared from nowhere, and then I guess he must have recognized me.'

'You know him?'

Quigley peered at the man on the ground.

'He might have been one of the bunch that attacked

Noreen and me that day at the ranch. He seemed to recognize me.'

'Which only proves this is more of the Circle M dirty work.'

'As if there were any doubt.'

'No harm done, anyway. I'll get back in position and we can fire up the show.'

Murray spurred away. Quigley threw the man's revolver far out into the night before recovering his slicker and climbing back on his horse. He heard a low whistle from Murray and decided it was time to go. Whooping loudly and flapping his slicker he rode towards the dozing cattle. They seemed reluctant to move, but a wave of restlessness was spreading though the herd as Murray did his own stint of chivvying them.

'Come on, you stubborn critters!' Quigley yelled.

He slapped a steer across the rear with his slicker and flapped the oilskin wildly in the air. The garment snapped and cracked as he rode up and down yelling. A steer bellowed in protest and there was a sudden surge away from the disturbance.

'Yeehaw!' came echoing out of the night as Murray gave vent to a rebel yell.

Quigley repeated the call. The cattle surged forwards, trying to get away from the boisterous beings in the night that made such terrifying noises.

'Yeehaw!'

And then the cattle were running, with the two riders yelling and flapping their capes behind them, giving them no let-up. The cattle fled in front of them and Quigley and Murray followed, racing their horses in the trail of the charging animals. Gradually they picked up speed and the thunder of hoofs drowned out all other sounds.

Quigley had no way of knowing where the rustlers were

in the midst of all this turmoil. He guessed they were scrambling for their horses and might attempt to turn the herd. But he reckoned they stood little chance of that in the darkness and confusion. Once the herd were running they would keep on going until tiredness slowed them. For all Quigley knew they might run all the way back to the Barrel B, and he grinned at the thought.

'Yeehaw!' he yelled again. And the herd thundered ahead of him and he followed, breathing in the dust they were kicking up in their mad, frantic dash.

17

Somewhere in the night Quigley heard gunshots and briefly pondered what they signified. He wondered if Murray had run into trouble, but he was too busy keeping up with the herd to do anything about it. He just hoped the cattle were running in the right direction.

When he lined up Murray and himself he had wanted to start the animals running on a course that would take them back towards the Barrel B. Pounding along in the wake of the stampeding cattle he had no idea how that was working out. For now, all he could do was stay with the herd. When daylight came or when the cattle ran out of steam, only then would he be able to get his bearings.

As the hours wore on, so too did Quigley feel the strain of keeping up with the herd. Every so often he would yell at the beasts as if to let them know he was still there and chasing them. But the brutal ride was taking its toll on rider and horse. He could feel the forward momentum of the runaway steers slowing, and tried to summon up another yell, but his throat was parched with the dust he was breathing and he could only produce a weak croak.

Briefly he thought of pulling his revolver and letting off a few shots, but decided against it. If the rustlers were following, as they most likely were, he did not want to draw them to him.

Slumped on top of his horse he kept going by sheer doggedness, peering through red-rimmed eyes but unable to make out very much. At some stage he might have fallen asleep, because he jerked upright with a start. A faint light was on the horizon, and he shook his head to clear it of the fog of drowsiness. He gazed around him but could see no other riders. There was just him and a herd of cattle plodding slowly forwards.

He got out his canteen and swigged water, gargling some and spitting some, easing the dryness of his throat. There was a yell and someone was riding towards him. Quigley pulled his gun and waited. There was something familiar about the dust-coated figure.

'Murray!' he called.

'Quigley, you made it then.'

'Am I glad to see you,' Quigley said. 'Even if you do look like the Grey Ghost.'

'You're sure making a good imitation yourself in that costume.'

Quigley glanced down, surprised by the coating of dust on his clothing and on his mount. The two sat atop their horses and grinned tiredly at each other.

'Well, we made it.'

'You have any trouble?'

'Run into some of those rustlers early on and had a shootout with them,' Murray answered. 'You?'

74

'Nah, not after that fella as jumped me. Once these steers were on the move I was on my lonesome. Just kept on moving.'

'How far you think we come?' Murray asked.

Quigley glanced up at the sky before answering.

'We've been travelling most of the night. If we kept on course we might be halfway. Maybe hit the home range sometime tonight. Right now I just want to fall off my horse and crawl in my bedroll and sleep for a week. But we got to keep going. If those rustlers are trailing us we'll be hard put to stave them off the condition I'm in.'

'Yeah, maybe you're right. We'll just have to soldier on.'

All that day they kept hazing the cows. The animals were tired and wanted to stop and graze or just rest. The two men rode their weary horses up and down the herd chivvying the beasts when they looked like slowing down. Not only were the horses weary, but also the men on top of them.

They waved their slickers and yelled until they were hoarse. It got to the stage that Quigley hardly had the energy to raise his arm to flap his slicker. He swopped to his left arm but even that gave out after constant movement. He tried to whistle, but hadn't the spit. Away over on his right he was aware of Murray working the cattle, and assumed he was as weary as he was. Quigley figured if the rustlers caught up with them they would have an easy time overrunning them and taking back the herd.

The cattle bawled and protested but kept moving. Occasionally one would just give up and lie down. There was nothing the herders could do about these – they couldn't risk a shot to put them out of their misery. Quigley hoped that they would perhaps rest up and eventually follow on.

After what seemed to be a whole lifetime driving weary

steers he heard someone shouting. He looked up, but couldn't see anyone. He squinted through red-rimmed eyes in an attempt to make out who was causing the disturbance. A rider was coming towards him. Instinctively he pulled his revolver.

'Quigley!'

'Noreen, where did you come from?' he called, feeling foolish as he returned his revolver to its holster.

She pulled up alongside him and frowned as she examined him.

'You look beat.'

He tried to grin, but failed. 'I guess you could say that. How did you get here?'

'When you didn't return I decided to ride out after you. I see you got the cattle back.'

'Yeah, most of them. Are we far from the ranch?'

'Another few miles and you're on home range.'

Quigley's shoulders drooped with fatigue, mixed with relief.

'Home range – those are the most welcome words I ever run across,' he said and repeated the phrase. 'Home range.'

Noreen saw immediately what had to be done, and rode past Quigley and used her voice to chivvy the herd.

'Hip, hip, hip! Come on fellas, you're nearly home. Only another mile or so and you can rest your weary hides.'

Quigley slumped in the saddle and closed his eyes, and listened to Noreen as she urged the cattle forwards.

'Hip, hip, hip!' she called, and Quigley felt some of the weariness drop from him.

Even the horse picked up the pace as Noreen, almost by her own efforts, drove the herd forwards.

'Hip, hip, hip!' she called, and whether it was because

the steers could sense they were nearly home or because of Noreen's hollering, it seemed they were moving at a slightly faster pace.

'Home range,' Quigley murmured, 'how sweet that sounds.'

18

That night after settling the cattle, which wouldn't be going anywhere soon, not after their traumatic couple of days, Quigley and Murray ate a hearty supper and then retired to bed. They went to bed early and rose late the next morning. There was no one about and they cooked a breakfast of ham and eggs.

'Wonder where everyone has got to?' Murray asked.

'Maybe out looking to the cattle,' replied Quigley. 'Got to be some casualties amongst them. They were hard driven for a day or so, and then stampeded. Hate to see cattle pushed like that.'

'Well, at least we managed to get them back.'

'We lost a head or two, I reckon. Saw a few go down during the stampede. Nothing I could do about that. We just had to keep on pushing. When I finish here I'll go out and lend a hand.'

'How d'you reckon this is all going to end?' Murray asked.

Quigley didn't answer immediately, but concentrated on building a cigarette. He blew a plume of smoke into the room, then sighed deeply.

'Look around you, Murray. We are sitting in a typical homesteader's dwelling. No ostentatious show of wealth. Functional furniture, simple fare served up at mealtimes. Peter Barker wanted to build a future for his family. He would work at increasing the size of his herd, maybe have a few more kids. As time went on the ranch would become more prosperous. He would hire a few hands to help them do the work. Noreen and he would educate their children – send them on to college. The Barker family would flourish in this little corner of Utah.'

Quigley fell silent, staring into the middle distance with pensive eyes.

'Sounds idyllic,' Murray said, 'and it would be, only for the wolves circling the homestead. Her princes in her midst thereof are like wolves ravening the prey, to shed blood, to destroy souls, to get dishonest gain. Ezekiel, Old Testament.'

Quigley squinted at his friend through the cigarette smoke, at the same time raising his eyebrows.

'I reckon you took up the wrong trade as lawman. You should have been a skypilot.'

'I suppose in a way it's a kind of similar job. A preacher seeks to keep the law of God, while the peace officer tries to maintain the law of the land. One does it with a Bible while the other does it with a gun.'

'Are you saying you do both – a Bible in one hand and a gun in the other?'

'I sure as hell attempt no such thing. I don't preachify to the drunken cowhand shooting up the town afore I clonk him on the head with my pistol and haul him off to jail. A fella has to draw the line somewhere.'

Quigley grinned back at him. Murray and he were more than deputy and sheriff: they were also good friends. He got up from the table.

'Much as I could sit here all day and shoot the breeze, I reckon I ought to get out there with Noreen and help with those cattle.'

'Let's do that.'

They saddled up and rode out. In a while they spotted the herd and drifted towards them. Sure enough they found Noreen tending a calf.

'This little fella lost its ma. I'm trying to match it up with a cow. No one seems interested. I guess they are all too tired.'

'Yeah, I know how they feel,' Quigley said. 'Anything we can do to help?'

'I'm looking for injured animals to see if I can help them. If you could go through the herd and bring out any as needs attention we can take them up near the house and keep an eye on them.'

'Sure thing,' Quigley said. He turned to Murray. 'Do you know which the front end and which the rear end is of a steer?'

'Sure thing. If it kind of matches your face then that has to be the rear end.'

Noreen tried to smother her guffaw and managed to turn it into a snort. Grinning at each other the two men rode through the herd on the lookout for sick or injured animals. At midday they rode back to the house for lunch. As they dismounted Quigley realized he hadn't seen Betsy or Jemima. When he quizzed Noreen about this she told him school had started and Betsy drove Jemima to school, where she also helped out.

'They'll be back this afternoon.'

They ate a cold lunch, and after quaffing several mugs of coffee rode back out to the herd to continue working. Ever conscious of the threat that faced them from McRae's roughnecks, the trio kept a lookout for riders. It was late in the afternoon when they decided to call it a day.

'I don't know how to thank you two,' Noreen said on the ride back. 'A few days ago with my herd gone I believed it was the end for me and the Barrel B. All things considered, the cattle are in reasonably good shape after their ordeal.'

'Probably more than you can say for your two new cowhands,' Murray quipped.

'I know!' Noreen flashed them a concerned look. 'It's been nothing but trouble for you since you arrived here. If you upped and rode out I wouldn't blame you.'

'And I say therefore unto ye, render to the widow and her orphan child all aid that they may not be stricken down by the wicked,' Murray intoned.

Noreen tried to blink away the tears that came then, and had to look away to hide her emotion. Quigley noted her behaviour and tried to lighten the mood.

'Beware the man who has a Bible verse at the drop of a hat.'

She wiped at her eyes and gave him a wan smile. They rode the remainder of the way in silence, weary after the day's toil, looking forward to a rest and a meal. When they got to the gate Jemima came out on the stoop and waved to them. They waved back and headed for the barn to tend to the horses.

'You go on and see to Jemima,' Quigley told Noreen. 'We'll take care of the horses.'

She smiled gratefully and left them to it. They busied themselves removing harness and feeding and rubbing down. After that, they sluiced away the dust of the day at the water barrel, then headed up to the house. As soon as Quigley came inside the house he sensed something had happened. Murray noticed it too and looked solemnly at the women. Noreen looked disconsolate, cradling Jemima on her knee and smoothing her hair. Betsy was by the stove preparing the evening meal. The little girl glanced up briefly as the men entered.

'Have a seat, boys,' Betsy called. 'Dinner won't be long.'

Quigley sat at the table while Murray walked over to Betsy.

'Can I help?' he asked.

When she looked at him he could see something was troubling her. Suddenly tears welled up. Murray instinctively put his arms around her.

'Stop it, you big bear,' she mumbled into his vest. 'Taking advantage of a poor defenceless woman.'

She made Murray go and sit down at the table. It was only when the dinner was served up and they were tucking in that she told them about her day at the school.

19

All had gone well until the school day finished, but when Betsy came out to drive Jemima home, she found the buckboard was gone. Not knowing what else to do, she went to the sheriff and reported the loss. His stock answer was that he would look into it. Betsy found herself stranded in town with no way of getting home.

She had two little girls with her, Jemima being one and her pal, Joanna Alkire. Betsy was wont to pick up the girl on her way to school and drop her off on the way back. The youngster came from a poor family and may not have been able to attend school but for the help given her by Jemima's family. In the end it was the teacher who came to the rescue. Sophronia Wineteer was the preacher's wife as well as being the school teacher. She hitched up her husband's buckboard and drove Betsy and the girls home.

'But now what happens?' Betsy asked. 'How do I get the children to school? I suppose if I have to, I could ride in on one of the saddle ponies, but I haven't been on a horse for years and I always rode side-saddle. I can't see me doing that for any length of time. And then there's the problem of transporting the children. If I could get my hands on the varmint as stole that buckboard I'd ... I'd ...'

She faded into silence, not sure if she could voice the dire punishment she had in mind for the thief. The little group chewed over the problem while they chewed on the prime steaks Betsy had cooked for them. It was Murray who came up with the solution.

'How's about I do the school run? Jemima can sit up front, and when I pick up her friend she can clamber up behind me. At least Jemima won't miss any schooling until we can either recover the buckboard or buy a new one.'

'You'd be willing to do that?' Betsy asked.

'Don't see why not. If Noreen agrees, and you, of course.'

'Thing is,' Betsy said, 'I help out in school.'

Murray's grin was as wide as a church door.

'I'm sure I can make myself useful. I can read and write better than some. And can count up to fifteen million.'

Jemima's eyes were wide as she took this in.

'Fifteen million,' she repeated. 'I bet you can't!'

'I can, too. I did it when I was five years old. When I finished counting I was a year older.'

No one could have stopped the laughter that bubbled

up when Murray said that. It lightened the mood of the women for the rest of the evening. It was only later when they were alone that Quigley got the chance to discuss the situation with Murray.

'If McRae's bullies are bold enough to steal Betsy's buggy then they sure as hell will try to bushwhack you. You want me to tag along tomorrow?'

'Nah, I'll be all right. Surely they'll not try anything in front of the kids.'

Next morning Murray set off on the school run with Jemima perched up in front of him and seeming pleased to do so. When they rode away from the ranch they left three very worried adults behind.

That night when the pair returned they were able to report there had been no trouble. Murray delivered the girls to the school and then rode to the livery to stable his horse for the day. He had quizzed the ostler about the theft of the Betsy's buckboard, but the man claimed he knew nothing about it.

'Must have happened when I was gettin' lunch. I go over to Parsnip Pete's. You should try it. Dang good chow, an' dog cheap too.'

It was the same everywhere he inquired. No one saw no one stealing no buckboard. So for the time being, Murray delivered the girls to school and stayed to help out. Mostly he read to some of the younger children.

Sophronia Wineteer, the woman in charge of the school, was at first wary of this big man who offered to help. Mistaking his size for roughness, she kept an eye on him during the school day. Mostly the children took to Murray, treating him as an amiable big playmate. And the schoolteacher had to admit that the big man was a decided asset to her establishment.

It wasn't until the third day that the thugs struck.

The school day was winding to a close, and Murray walked over to the livery. He set about saddling and bridling his horse. Usually the ostler was somewhere about, but today he was missing. As Murray worked on the harness he heard someone come inside the building. Thinking it was the liveryman, Murray turned around. He counted five as they filed inside, and knew exactly what they had come for. They were taking their time: mean-eyed, vicious killers, sent to deal with the upstart who had dared come to the aid of the Barker women. The last man in turned and closed the big wooden doors.

'*Lord,*' Murray prayed as he eyed up the gunnies lining up in front of him, '*You weren't too proud to be born in a stable. I don't want to die in a stable, but maybe you fixed it so as I would. But I'd sure appreciate it if I survived to take care of those little girls as you put in my care.*'

With a quick movement Murray smacked the horse across the rump. The animal jumped, snorted and plunged away from him towards the men sent to deal with him. They scattered as the startled horse blundered in amongst them.

While they were so distracted Murray snatched up a piece of timber used as a drop bar on the stall doors. With a couple of strides he reached the group scrambling to dodge the panicked horse.

He felled his first victim with a sideways swipe to the side of the head, sending him stumbling into one of his companions. Another, seeing what was happening, pulled his gun, but before he could fire, the timber baton broke his arm as Murray smashed it with his club. The gun went off and a man yelled as the bullet hit him in the leg. Then Murray was in amongst the gang, laying about him with his makeshift club.

Murray was a big, muscular man, and when he delivered a blow with that heavy piece of timber it inevitably broke bones. He showed no mercy as he set about his work with relish. These bullies had been sent to kill him – probably the same men as had beaten his pal, Quigley. Now was time for payback.

Clunk! A man's jaw was broken as the wooden baton hit him and knocked him against the wall. Wham! Fingers were broken as they vainly attempted to ward off that swinging timber. Yells and curses and screams as the gunnies scrambled to get away from the Goliath that waded amongst them, breaking bones and heads with obvious enthusiasm.

A knee was jolted out of its socket and as the victim opened his mouth to yell, the timber smashed into his face. A shot blasted out as a gunman got his weapon up, missing the intended target. Murray threw the baton like a javelin, causing the man to duck, but it struck him on the shoulder and then Murray was upon him, kicking him in the chest. The stricken man stumbled to the floor with several broken ribs, finding it hard to breath. Murray stomped his gun hand into the dirt, his boot crushing the bones to pulp.

Retrieving his makeshift weapon the big man went through the injured men and cracked each one on the head to make sure they stayed down and out. Finally he stood back and surveyed his work.

'I guess I weren't born to die in no stable, Lord. To thee I give thanks for my delivery.'

For the next while Murray busied himself stripping the men of weapons and tossing them up into the loft. Then he dragged the unconscious men inside a stall. Using lariats he roped them together. Closing the door on the trussed men he wedged the bar in place and went to calm his horse standing quivering in a corner.

'Sorry old fella, I had to have an edge. You did well. When we get back tonight I'm going to give you extra carrot and maybe an apple. What d'ya say? You forgive me?'

Talking soothingly, he tightened the harness and led the horse outside. The ostler was perched on the edge of the water trough, smoking. He turned with a smirk when he heard the door open, but his mouth fell open when he saw who emerged. He stood up abruptly, his cigarette momentarily forgotten.

'You . . . what. . . ?' he stuttered.

It was then that Murray knew the liveryman was complicit in the attack. He strode over. The man cowered back, but Murray grabbed him by his shirt front.

'You son of a bitch, you were in on this,' he growled. 'You probably know who took Mrs Gallagher's buckboard.'

'I know nothing,' the man squealed. 'I told you afore.'

Murray lifted the man and dumped him in the trough. The liveryman flopped about wildly, spilling water and going under. As he came up gasping, Murray's big hand gripped him again.

'Where is that goddamn buckboard?'

Spewing up water and gasping for air, the man shook his head and burbled something unintelligible. Murray pushed him under and this time held him down. The water frothed and spilled as the man struggled for release. He stood no chance as that big hand held him as easy as if he were a chicken. As the man's struggles weakened Murray hauled him up again.

'Now tell me where that goddamn buckboard is or I swear I'll drown you.'

The man pointed feebly towards the side of the stables. Murray lugged him out. His legs gave way, but Murray grabbed him and dragged him in that direction. There was a large outbuilding, and hauling his waterlogged sufferer in his wake, Murray strode over to it. Throwing open a door he saw the buckboard partially covered in canvas. He tossed the man inside and manoeuvred the vehicle out into the open. Once he had harnessed his horse between the shafts, Murray drove back to the schoolyard.

20

'They can't let that lie,' Quigley said as they sat on the porch after dinner that night. 'You take that buckboard into town and they're going to come at you, maybe this time in bigger numbers, or more than likely they'll send Slater to arrest you.'

'I guess that is how it's going to be,' Murray agreed. 'It's a fine state of affairs when a couple of kids can't get to school because of a goddamn vendetta.'

Quigley sighed deeply and blew smoke into the night. The door opened behind them and Noreen emerged.

'Murray, I'm sorry to disturb you, but Jemima wants you to read her a story. I tried to talk her out of it. Told her you were tired after all that teaching and stuff, but she is persisting. I'm sorry to bother you.'

'That ain't no bother, ma'am. It'll be my pleasure to read to her. I sure do love that little madam.'

Murray got up to go back inside. Noreen put out her hand to him.

'Thank you for everything, Murray. You're a wonderful

man, but would you please call me Noreen? When you call me "ma'am" I feel like an old lady.'

Murray flashed a big grin. 'Sure thing, Noreen.' And went inside the house.

Noreen sat on the vacated rocker.

'How is Jemima holding up with all this upset?' Quigley asked her.

'She misses her pa. I get the feeling Murray is a substitute. He's big and warm and lovable. No child could resist him.' She was silent for a moment before continuing. 'Once more I can only say how sorry I am that you have been drawn into this feud. I fear there will be only one ending to this, and that will be that either you or Murray, or both, will be murdered. I would never forgive myself. I have decided to sell up and leave. McRae has won.'

'You have nothing to be sorry for. None of this is of your making. Cruel and avaricious men are behind all that has happened to you. When they attacked me they made it personal. Your leaving will make no difference to me. I will see them brought to justice.'

'I . . . I thought that when I told you of my decision to leave, you would leave also.'

'I can't ride away from this.'

'You could go back to Idlereach and continue your life and forget all this.' She fell silent. Some moments passed before she spoke again. 'What did you do before you came here? You never actually said.'

'I was Sheriff of Idlereach – still am, and Murray is my deputy. When I put that badge on, I made an oath to uphold the law. I arrested the men as murdered your husband. I now suspect Peter's death was orchestrated from here. That being the case, this goes well beyond a local dispute. They came on my turf and committed a crime. I'm obligated to resolve this, whatever the consequences. Your decision to leave will have no bearing on the case or my future actions. But I heartily approve. This is no place to bring up a family.'

She was staring at him, but the light was fading and she couldn't see his face.

'I understand now. That's why you came out here to tell me about Peter.'

In the darkness she could hear his long drawn-out sigh.

'At the time I believed it was a plot against my own life, and Peter was just an innocent pawn the killers were using to draw me into their trap. I had a history with the men involved. Since then my views have changed, and I now believe they were given a contract on your husband. My arrival here threatened to expose that connection and so they decided to discourage me by giving me that hiding and leaving me to die. Now it has gone beyond that. After all that has happened, McRae will do his utmost to stop me and Murray permanently. McRae has declared war against me. I can turn tail and run, or I can stay on and fight back.'

'But there are only two of you. McRae has immense wealth and dozens of men. This is foolish. Why throw your life away?'

'What would you have us do? Ride away and forget all that has happened? These varmints murdered your husband – they beat me near to death – they steal your buckboard – they steal your cattle – they attack Murray – they interfere with Jemima's schooling. They do whatever they want with impunity. If they've done all that to one family, what have they not done to countless others? I don't think I could live with myself if I rode away.

'What would have happened to our proud nation if our forefathers had abandoned fairness and justice? They fought for freedom in the War of Independence and again during the recent war amongst the states. The scum that run Gila County have thrashed all those proud aspirations. They are riding roughshod over our laws and freedoms. The fourteenth amendment of our constitution states that no person is to be deprived of life, liberty or property without the due process of law. These people need to be brought to justice. No one is above the law.'

Noreen was staring across at him, her forehead wrinkled in a frown.

'What are you going to do?' she asked.

'I'm not sure yet,' he said. 'I'll sleep on it.'

But he knew already what he had to do. His mind was made up. Betsy came out with a tray of mugs and a steaming coffee pot.

'Drinks anyone? I baked some hot cakes.'

Quigley sighed. For now he would enjoy the good company and home cooking provided by the women of the ranch. Tomorrow was another day. What was it that Noreen had quoted him from Shakespeare? He only remembered part of it. But he didn't like to ask her to repeat it. Something about tomorrow, and tomorrow, and tomorrow, and lighted fools and dusty death!

21

In the morning after breakfast Murray helped Betsy with harnessing up the buckboard. While he was doing so, Quigley was also busy, saddling up two mounts.

'Are you thinking of riding in with us?' Betsy asked.

'No, we'll be coming in later,' Quigley told her.

'Do you think they'll try anything?' she asked.

'Hard to tell. After Murray gave them that thrashing they might sit back and lick their wounds for a day or two. Noreen seems to think they won't harm you or the children – just make things difficult for you.'

'What – like stealing the buckboard?'

'Yeah! But now we know the liveryman was implicated in the theft, he might be leery of getting involved again.'

'Humph! What's he got to be leery of? Sheriff Slater won't do anything.'

'That's something that's been bothering me some. Slater is the worst kind of lawman. He's more interested in guarding the law breakers than he is in protecting the law-abiding.'

Noreen came out with Jemima, and Murray handed the girl up into the buckboard. Jemima spotted Quigley leading the saddled horses out of the stables.

'Oh, good,' she said, 'You're coming with us.'

The big man grinned up at her.

'Not today, young 'un. Today you have a nice comfortable ride in the buckboard with your grandma.'

'Oooh!' Jemima pouted in disappointment.

Betsy was grinning across at Murray. 'Seems a ride perched on the neck of your horse is more welcome than a comfy ride with her long-suffering grandma.' She flicked the reins and drove the buckboard out of the yard. 'Bye!'

'When I saw you saddling up I thought you would be riding in with Betsy,' Noreen said.

'Nah, that might be too much provocation. You told us McRae wouldn't hurt the females of this ranch. No, I reckon Betsy and Jemima will be safe enough for now. We have other cats to whip.'

'What! What the hell does that mean?'

He gave her a lopsided grin. 'Language, Mrs Barker!' Quigley swung up on his horse.

'Quigley, what are you up to?'

He waved and rode out of the yard, followed by Murray who nodded to Noreen as he followed Quigley. She was left staring after them with anxiety gnawing at her innards.

The two men rode easily, seemingly not in any hurry. The sun was low on the horizon with a slight mistiness rising up from the ground. Quigley wrapped the reins around his saddle horn and took out his makings. While he rolled the smoke he thought about what he was about to do. He glanced across at Murray. The big man was looking at him.

'Them smokes will kill you some day,' he called.

'A man got to die of something. Are you sure you want to go through with this, Murray? There's still time to change your mind.'

'When did I ever ask you to stir my porridge, Quigley? Whatever your hand finds to do, do it with all your might, for there is no work or thought or knowledge or wisdom in Slimwater, to which you are going.'

Quigley got his smoke alight before saying anything. 'I don't recall that particular verse in the Bible.'

'Ecclesiastes, only I swopped Slimwater for Sheol.'

Quigley burst out laughing. 'I never know if you really know the Good Book that well, or if you just make it up as you go along.'

'One of the great mysteries of life, Quigley. A man versed in the ways of the Lord shall shine like a beacon for all eternity.'

Quigley gave Murray a sardonic look and got a grin in return. After that they rode towards Slimwater in silence. They wanted Betsy to arrive well in advance of them and maybe distract attention from their own arrival in the town.

The morning mist had vanished when eventually they sighted the town. They rode steadily past the town boundaries and pulled up outside the post office. Quigley handed his reins to Murray. His task was to keep a lookout for Slater and his deputies while Quigley conducted his business inside.

At the sight of his customer the clerk paled. Wordlessly Quigley slid his message on to the counter. There was a slight tremor in the man's hand as he read the content. His eyes widened and he stared at Quigley in consternation.

'You're a lawman,' he stuttered.

'Just send the message.'

The clerk gulped, but did as he was told.

'If I find that communication gets leaked, then I'm coming back here and you will spend a long time contemplating your misdeeds in the penitentiary. As a matter of fact I might just arrest you anyway.'

The clerk's mouth opened and closed but no sound came out. Hoping he had done enough to prevent his plans from becoming known to his enemies, Quigley paid the few cents fee.

'When you get a reply, send it down the sheriff's office. That's where you'll more than likely find me.'

Leaving a very frightened clerk behind, Quigley went back out into the street. Murray shook his head to let Quigley know he had not spotted any trouble. They led the horses along the street to the law office. Here they repeated the same procedure. While Murray tied up the horses Quigley pushed open the door and stepped inside.

He recognized the deputies playing cards on a bench in a corner. He had cause to remember. They were amongst the gang that beat him last time he had visited Slimwater. Slater was at a desk leafing through some documents. He glanced up and his eyes widened as he recognized his visitor.

'Son of a bitch!' he yelled and went for his gun.

Quigley was expecting such a move and he was across the intervening space in a couple of long strides, pulling his gun as he moved. Sitting down, Sheriff Slater was at a disadvantage. Before he could get his gun out Quigley was on him. He swung his pistol and the barrel cracked against Slater's forehead, rocking him back in his chair. The deputies, seeing what was happening, went for their irons. Quigley hauled the dazed sheriff from the chair and using him as a shield, yelled at the men to drop their guns.

'You want a dead sheriff? Go ahead and start shooting.'

The deputies hesitated and Quigley shoved his gun up under Slater's chin, pushing so forcefully the lawman's head was bent back so he was staring at up at the ceiling.

'Damn you,' he croaked.

'Tell them – tell them to shed those irons else they got a dead sheriff on their hands.'

'Do it . . .' Slater wheezed.

But the taller of the two deputies must have thought he was a crack shot, for he took a chance and fired off a round. It was close, and the bullet stung Quigley's ear. He yelled out and using his shoulder shoved the sheriff towards the two men. Slater stumbled and fell to his knees. Quigley dropped behind the desk as the second deputy joined in the shooting and bullets thudded into the wood and whistled past his head.

Resting his hand on the desk, Quigley emptied his pistol at the two gunmen. At that distance a marksman like Quigley could not miss. Both men stumbled back, guns suddenly drooping towards the floor as bullets punched holes in them; their lifeless bodies toppled to the floor, blood leaking from several wounds, leaving crimson stains on the boards. The door was shoved open and Murray burst inside, gun at the ready.

'Quigley!' he yelled and stopped as he saw the carnage.

Slowly Quigley stood, punching spent shells from his gun.

'You all right?' Murray asked.

'Damn fellas must have had a death wish,' Quigley growled.

Sheriff Slater stayed on the floor with head bowed.

'Let's get this fella in a cell.'

Once the sheriff was safely locked up, Quigley found writing materials and wrote out a notice.

'Let's get these fellas outside.'

When Quigley opened the front door he saw people gathering in the street, drawn to the jail by the sounds of gunfire. He stood on the boardwalk and addressed the crowd.

'It's all right, folks,' Quigley called. 'Everything's under control.' He showed them the badge he had pinned on that morning. 'I'm taking over as sheriff for now. The last one you had wasn't fit for purpose. He's in a cell now awaiting justice.'

There was a low murmuring from the crowd.

'Has McRae ordered this?' a bearded man in a suit called. Quigley didn't answer.

'You can bet he did,' a cowboy said. 'Nothing happens in this town without McRae's say-so.'

The new lawmen placed the bench where the deputies had been playing cards out on the boardwalk. Together they dragged the dead men outside and arranged the lifeless bodies on the bench. Quigley pinned his notice on the chest of the man who had first shot at him. The notice read: 'These men abused their position as law officers. Instead of keeping the law they broke it and helped criminals escape justice.' It was signed 'Sheriff Quigley'.

'Go and fetch us some grub,' Quigley told Murray. 'Enough for a couple of days. We might be here for a while.'

22

When Murray returned he was carrying a couple of gunnysacks loaded with canned and packaged foodstuffs.

'This should keep us going,' he said. 'Goddamn storekeeper didn't want to serve me. I had to put him right on that.' The big man grinned. 'I made him give me a discount to make up for his unmannerly behaviour.' Murray dumped the food on the desk. 'I see you been busy and got the coffee on the go.'

'Yep, the mugs didn't look too clean but I swilled them out with hot water.'

'What about ammo?'

'Slater has some stored and I found a gunnysack of ammo I bought the day they buffaloed me. I wondered what had happened to that.' He poured another coffee. 'I'd better take Slater a cup of java. Don't want him to feel neglected.'

He found Slater lying on the bunk. He didn't get up when Quigley appeared. The new sheriff reached the mug through the bars and set it on the floor.

'You're going to die for this,' Slater said, his voice filled with bile. 'If you let me go, I'll give you the chance to ride out of here. Otherwise you are heading for a bullet or a rope.'

'You could be right. I never wanted any part of this. A dying man asked me to deliver a message to his widow. I carried out my bounden duty and delivered that message. Almost immediately I was attacked by Virgil McRae. Next thing you waylay me and beat me near to death. I kind of got to wondering what sort of set-up there was here, that made me such a threat. Then it began to come together.

'McRae ordered the killing of Peter Barker. I guess he thought that by having him killed so far from home no one would make the connection. Slimwater, and everyone connected to McRae, is rotten to the core. And you, Slater, who took an oath to uphold law and order, are the worst kind of vermin crawling through the slime along with him. So think on your defence when you come to trial for mis-using the office entrusted to you.'

'There won't be any trial. McRae will come in here and pull this place apart. And if you survive that, which I doubt, he'll drag you out and hang you. I'll be only too pleased to haul on the rope. That much I can guarantee you – death by a bullet or death by a rope.'

'You want a doctor to look at that head of yours. It looks pretty nasty. Pity it didn't knock some sense into you.'

'Do what the hell you like,' Slater snarled. 'You ain't got much time left afore they come for you.'

Quigley went back to the front office. Murray was checking the various weapons stored by Slimwater's lawmen.

'Well,' he said, 'we got plenty of firepower. What we lack is a plan and manpower.'

'A plan!' Quigley had a sardonic look on his face as he spoke. 'Oh, I forgot to tell you. This is the plan. McRae will send his gun hounds in to root us out. I figure anything from twenty to thirty. I will ask them to surrender or face the consequences. Simple plans are the best.'

Someone knocked on the door. Immediately both men had guns in their hands.

'Come in,' Quigley called.

The door opened and a youngster, no more than eight to nine years old, came inside. He had an envelope in his hand. His eyes widened as he saw the guns. Quickly the weapons disappeared.

'Howdy, son. You got a message for me?'

'Yessir!'

He held out the envelope. Quigley took it from him.

'What's your name, son?' he asked, as he opened the message.

'Glen, sir.'

Quigley scanned the paper. He dug in his pocket and handed the boy a quarter.

'There you go, Glen. You take care now.'

The boy's eyes widened as he looked at the coin.

'Gee thanks, mister. I got to go to school now, but I can come back after school if you have any more errands.'

His freckled face stared earnestly up at Quigley.

'No, I don't think that would be a good idea,' Quigley said. The boy looked so disappointed Quigley had a change of heart. 'Tell you what. If I need you I'll leave a message at the post office.'

'Yessir! Thank you, sir.'

When he was gone out the door Quigley turned to Murray and held up the paper.

'As you know I sent that telegram to Judge Leyman Updegrove telling him I was provisionally taking over as sheriff here, and requesting he send a team of marshals to investigate the malpractices of the law officers in

98

Slimwater.'

Quigley looked down at the paper then handed it to his companion.

'Regret unable accede to request,' Murray read. 'Ongoing cases have left me with inadequate forces. Try me in a week's time or two.' He glanced up at Quigley. 'We're on our own, then.'

'Looks that way.'

'Perhaps you moved a mite premature. A week or two is a long time.'

'A week or two is a long time, as you say. Maybe we better revise our plans.'

'You did have a plan. You were just holding out on me.'

Quigley grinned across at his companion.

'The plan was to hold out here until Updegrove's marshals arrived. I thought we had a few days grace. Now it looks like we have a mite longer to hold out. Trouble is, I figure we can't hold out for that length of time.'

'So what then? We've started the bush fire. How we going to put it out?'

'Before that message I was figuring you and I could hole up here until help arrived. We got food and ammo aplenty. In the light of no help arriving, we wouldn't be able to survive a determined attack much beyond the couple of days I reckoned on. I figure we got until sometime tonight, or at most tomorrow, afore they make a move against us. After that it would only be a matter of time afore they overwhelm us.'

'So we're dead men if we sit tight, and dead men if we make a run for it.'

Quigley narrowed his eyes and stared back at his deputy.

'I know that look, Quigley. If I'm not mistaken something's cooking in that noggin of yours.'

'Someone once said, the best means of defence is attack,' Quigley said thoughtfully. 'Right now we got to play a little game of deception. Keep an eye out front in case we're wrong and the Circle M decides to come early afore we make our move.'

He walked into the cellblock. The empty coffee mug was set on the floor. Sheriff Slater scowled.

'My damn head hurts. I need a doctor.'

'You said earlier you would give me a chance to ride away,' Quigley said.

'Yeah!'

Quigley handed Slater the telegraph. The sheriff scanned the note.

'I thought I would have help coming,' Quigley said. 'But now it looks as if I'm on my own. If I release you, I need your word you'll give me a half a day's riding afore you raise the alarm.'

A slow smile spread across the sheriff's face.

'Son of a bitch, I'll give you your half day. But I can't guarantee Mr McRae will honour that pledge.'

'Afore we leave I'll drop the key of your cell with the doctor. Tell him to release you. I trust you to keep your word and give us that half day afore sending anyone after us.'

23

Once again Quigley was riding away from Slimwater, this time not back to the Barrel B, but retracing the path he had taken when he first arrived in the area. Beside him rode his deputy and friend Murray Fishbourne. Their route skirted the massive Mammoth Heights, dark and brooding on the skyline. They rode in silence for the most part, taking their time, conserving their mounts as if they had a long trail ahead.

'You regret coming out here, Quigley?' Murray asked.

Quigley fished out the makings and began fashioning a cigarette before replying.

'Well, I do confess I would much rather be back in Idlereach doing what I normally do. Idlereach ain't such a bad town to police. After I cleaned out the scum that were running wild in the eastern side of town, things settled down a mite. Drunken cowboys letting off steam, the odd shooting incident, watching out for gunnies drifting into town looking for trouble. Other than that it wasn't a bad job. From time to time I could have a day off to go fishing, while you minded the shop. So, do I regret coming here? No, I don't reckon I do. When I took the oath to uphold law and order it bit home. So when I arrive here and find this whole rotten mess, it sours my belly. And then I take it a mite personal when people try to kill me. What about you? You have any regrets?'

'I think you said it all. It is easier for the heavens and the earth to pass than one tittle of the law to fail.' He saw Quigley turn towards him, but before he could speak, beat him to it. 'I know what you are going to ask. Did I make it up? No, it is a verse from the apostle Luke.'

Quigley raised his eyebrows. 'No, that ain't what I was going to say. I was wondering what a tittle is?'

'Huh! You know, I never thought about that. Tittle, mmm . . . I guess it might be a titmouse's chick, you know a tiny tit. They ain't much bigger than a bumble bee.'

Quigley was shaking his head, a wide grin on his face. After a while they quartered west and rode for an hour or so before spotting a low hillock covered in oak trees and scraggy sage.

'Let's get to the top of that and see what is to be seen. If my calculations are right I reckon we must be pretty close to the McRae ranch.'

Once on the top they reined in and could see in the distance a jumble of buildings. Quigley fished for his glass and a bunch of keys tumbled out.

'Them the keys to the jail?' Murray asked, watching while Quigley pushed them back in his saddle-bag.

'Yep, I told Slater I would give them to the sawbones so he could release him and treat his head where I belted him.'

'But you didn't – you didn't give the keys to the sawbones?'

'Well, I figured as soon as Slater got out he would send a message to McRae to tell him we were hightailing it. This would mean that McRae would send his hounds out here after us, which is not where I want them.'

As he spoke Quigley had his eye to the glass. Slowly he scanned the surrounding countryside, seeing a seemingly unending vista of purple sage broken by the odd clump of trees. Almost everywhere he looked cattle could be seen in clusters. There didn't appear to be any cowboys tending the livestock. He wondered if they had been pulled off the range so they could take part in the raid on Slimwater to deal with Murray and himself.

Quigley was hoping his ploy had worked and that the raid would go ahead. If McRae still believed his quarry was in town holding Slater in jail, then he would send his hellions into town to free the sheriff and deal with the troublesome lawmen from Idlereach.

'We'll hunker down here a while and wait for things to develop,' he told Murray.

'What is there to develop?'

'I'm hoping McRae sends his gunhands on a wild goose chase into Slimwater, which means there won't be many left behind. Then we go down and pay the good rancher a visit.'

'Beelzebub's bells, Quigley, you're taking one hell of a chance riding down there into the lion's den. I guess you been smoking peyote mixed in with that Bull Durham. A man like McRae will have so many enemies he'll be surrounded by bodyguards at all times. How do you think he's survived all these years?'

'Probably during all those years, McRae never had no one challenge him and so he most likely has become fat and complacent. He'll be sitting down there issuing orders, feeling safe in his den, as you call it. I'll ride down there and take him completely by surprise. I'll arrest him and take him to Templeton where Judge Updegrove can try him. Maybe by then the judge will have marshals to spare as he can send down here to tidy things up and take Slater into custody.'

'I always had faith in your judgement, Quigley, but this smacks of recklessness.' Murray was shaking his head as he spoke. 'I got a bad feeling about it all.'

'Well, you can sit up here and watch. If I get in trouble, you head for Templeton and Judge Updegrove and come back and rescue me.'

'You damn fool, it'll be too late by then. They'll have you plucked and skinned and roasted well afore I get back from Templeton. And will that ole judge even listen to me?'

'Hang on!' Quigley put his glass to his eye again. 'Well, well, well, looks like something is happening down there.'

He could see a lot of activity around the corral. As he watched a sizeable body of riders rode away from the ranch, travelling towards Slimwater.

'There they go. They took the bait after all.'

He walked back to his horse and mounted. Murray quickly mounted up also.

'You're a mule-headed son of a bitch,' he grumbled. 'And you'll need me along to take care of you.'

'No, I need you out here to stay free if anything goes wrong. Remember what I told you. Head for Templeton and let Judge Updegrove handle things from there.'

Murray watched Quigley start down the slope in the direction of the Circle M ranch house. The bad feelings he had about this whole venture refused to abate.

'Lord, if you're listening,' he prayed, 'look after that brave but foolish man, and shield him under the shadow of thy wings.'

24

The yard was deserted as Quigley rode in, which suited him perfectly. It confirmed McRae had taken the bait and stripped his ranch of manpower in order to deal with Murray and himself and to rescue Slater.

He rode up to the house, a long, single-storey dwelling, built in stone and with a veranda running the full length. The portico was supported by whole tree trunks spaced at intervals. Quigley dismounted and was about to ascend the steps when he had an afterthought. Taking one of the pistols he had found in Slater's office, a Smith & Wesson Model 3 Russian, from under his coat, he wedged it under the saddle bag. He then mounted the steps and knocked on the door, hand on his holstered Colt.

'Come on in,' a voice called.

Quigley pushed open the door and stepped inside. The room was wide and deep, and the walls were lined with pine boards. Various animal skins and hides were scattered about the pine-board floor, and what must have been the heads to match were mounted on the walls. A log fire was built in the huge stone grate, but hadn't been lit. Behind a large oak desk sat a man Quigley guessed was the ranch owner.

'Howdy, what can I do for you?'

'I've come to see Huston McRae.'

'Well, you are looking at him.'

McRae was a narrow-faced man with long dark hair and a close-cropped beard, both lightly peppered with grey.

'I'm Sheriff Quigley from out of Idlereach.'

'Yeah, I figured that.'

'I'm here to arrest you,' Quigley said, his eyes narrowing as he watched the man at the desk, wondering how the hell McRae came to be expecting him, and wondering too, if he had a weapon concealed somewhere – his own hand resting on his gun.

'Have a seat, Mr Quigley. We have a lot to talk about. Would you like coffee or a cigar perhaps?'

'Maybe you didn't hear what I said. I'm here to arrest you.'

'Tut, tut, tut, Mr Quigley. Let's be realistic. You are here in my county, in my house and where you have no authority. How far do you think you would get if you tried to carry out your foolish threat? No, I have a better proposition.'

McRae paused in his speech while he reached over the desk. Quigley tensed, his hand tightening on his gun butt. The rancher lifted the lid of a humidor and extracted a long slim cigar.

'Are you sure you won't have one?'

Quigley surely would have liked a cigar, but he resisted.

'Time for talk is over,' he said. 'Get your coat. You're coming with me.'

'Well you see, that is what I want to discuss with you, if you would just relax and take your hand away from that gun.' Using a guillotine, McRae deftly snipped the end of the cigar. He smiled across at Quigley. 'I used to bite the end, but my wife, God rest her soul, introduced me to more refined ways. Now where were we? Yes, my proposition. What do you say to taking on the office of Sheriff of Slimwater? The salary is generous, a hundred a month plus expenses, and the duties not onerous.'

McRae paused and raised his eyebrows, waiting. Quigley blinked. A hundred a month was three times what he was earning as Sheriff of Idlereach, and out of that he had to buy ammunition and stabling for his horse. As he waited for Quigley's response, the rancher picked up a Lucifer, holding it up in the air between finger and thumb as if reluctant to light up before he got an answer.

'What about Slater? He ain't going to be too happy about being replaced.'

'Slater does as he's told.'

'How do you know I won't arrest you after I get the job?'

'Oh, that would mean you broke the terms of your employment and I would have to get rid of you.'

'Enough of this. Stand up and move away from the desk. We'll walk across to the corral and get you a horse. Then you and me are riding out of here.'

McRae nodded slowly. 'What part of my offer didn't you like?'

'It is easier for heaven and earth to pass than one tittle of the law to fall.'

With a flick of his thumbnail McRae ignited the match

and held the flame to his cigar. Several things happened then. The door behind Quigley opened, McRae disappeared behind that big desk, while other doors in the room opened and men with drawn guns spilled inside.

Quigley swivelled, pulling his gun. A pickaxe handle hit him on the shoulder. He staggered back, trying to bring his gun into action, but his arm refused to obey. Before he could get the gun lined up his feet were kicked from under him. He fired into the room, not aiming at anything, just shooting in the hope of hitting someone. There came another stunning blow from that hickory handle. His head bounced on the floor, not on one of the soft skins, but on the hard boards. He fired again, and gasped as a boot stamped on the hand holding the gun. He kicked out at the legs surrounding him. Someone laughed and plucked his gun from his bruised hand. It spun across the room.

Rough hands grabbed him and pulled him to his feet. Quigley struggled against them but those brutal blows with the pickaxe handle had sapped his strength. The man with the hickory handle rammed the end into his midriff. Quigley's mouth opened as the air was driven from him. His legs were weak and he would have fallen, only brutal hands were holding him upright. A fist hit him in the face and the hickory handle was rammed into his kidneys. He was floating in and out of consciousness hardly able to breathe, mouth open wide as he tried to suck in air.

'Enough!'

Into his blurred sight a figure moved to stand before him. A bearded face with a cigar in his mouth loomed up and blew out a plume of aromatic smoke into his face. Quigley tried to focus but there was too much pain rippling through his abused body. His vision blurred.

'Sheriff Quigley, you must understand that around

here, I am the law.'

More smoke in his face. He tried to breathe, but coughed instead. Fighting for breath.

'I am the law, the judge, the jury, and the executioner. I pronounce sentence upon you. You will be taken from this place into Mammoth Heights and there a hole will be prepared for you. I believe you quoted a piece of scripture earlier. Here's one for you. And if a man be stubborn in not obeying his elders he shall be taken from hence to a barren place and there stones will be placed upon his breast until his breath be stopped.'

Another plume of smoke wreathing around his face. Gasping and feeling the pain and the hopelessness of his situation. Rough hands gripping him and propelling him out the door. A cuff on the back of the head with something hard. Stars drifting in his vision. Hands lifting him up, seating him on the saddle.

'Goodbye, Sheriff Quigley. Enjoy your trip,' Huston McRae called from the veranda. 'You should have taken my offer.'

A rider gathered up the reins of Quigley's horse. He slumped across the neck of his mount, grimly holding on, fighting to stave off the fog in his mind and the dark void that threatened to engulf him. Five more gunhands joined them as he was led out of the yard.

25

The horsemen rode a long way into the hills. For most of the time they rode in silence. They climbed higher and higher, crossing rocky slopes penetrating into the mountain. After some time they reined up on the edge of a ravine.

'Hell, I think this is far enough.'

Far below, at the bottom of the chasm, Quigley could hear rushing water.

'Shoot him and toss him in the river.'

'Hell no! You know McRae. If his body washes up somewhere and he finds out, we're in big trouble. No, we can't risk it. We got to do as he says. We have to bury him under a pile of rocks.'

'Yeah, I guess you're right. We'll ride along the edge of this canyon until we find a good place where we can bury this knucklehead.'

'We find a hole and roll rocks on him! Do we have to kill him first or bury him alive?'

'I'd be more fun to chuck him in the hole and throw the rocks down on him. Listen to him screaming. Maybe we could do a little knifework on him. Carve him up a mite. See who can make him holler the most.'

'I prefer a hot iron myself. Not many can hold out against a red-hot iron in the eye or in the ear.'

Discussing the most painful way of disposing of their victim, the horsemen reined about and rode along the line of the ravine. During the ride Quigley had stayed slumped over the neck of his mount, gradually feeling his strength returning and weighing up his options. Surreptitiously he slid his hand down and located the gun he had wedged under the saddle-bags.

He did not rate his survival very high in a gunfight with so many ranged against him, but he would have the element of surprise. No one was taking much notice of him, their attention focused on finding a suitable spot to dispose of their victim.

He had the gun ready, hidden underneath his body. One of his captors held his lead rope and Quigley considered taking him out first and in the confusion making a break for it. While he was considering his options the party reined up before a shallow cleft.

'This'll do. Find some wood and get a fire going. I got a branding iron in my saddle-bags. We can burn him some and have an Arbuckle while we listen to him holler.'

They were preparing to dismount, and that was when Quigley made his move. Unnoticed by his captors he brought the gun came up from beneath his body. It was only feet from his target and he put a bullet into the man holding his lead rope. The gunnie yelled, and arched his back as the slug hammered into him. The wounded man flung his arms wide, involuntarily letting go the lead rope.

Lulled into complacency, because their victim had shown no signs of revival, the riders were grabbing for guns, but hampered at the same time by their horses stamping around, startled by the sudden gunshot. Quigley's own mount shied away, and he had a difficult time controlling it. He was also conscious of the edge of the ravine close by.

While the men wrestled with spooked mounts and pulling their guns, there was a sudden intrusion: a rifle shot blasted out and a gunman jerked back as a bullet hit him in the shoulder. Suddenly the whole scenario changed as an unknown marksman laid a barrage of shots into the group of horsemen.

Quigley realized there was a shooter out there taking pot-shots at his captors, and he had a fair idea as to who it might be. All thoughts of escape were gone. He slid from his panicked horse, and steadying himself with his feet braced, he brought his gun up and pumped a shot into the nearest rider. The stricken man curled over the horn of his saddle and kicked his horse with his spurs in an attempt to escape the gunfire. Quigley shot him again, and as the horse pranced sideways the man was dumped from the saddle.

The hidden rifleman was shooting steadily, and another two men were hit. One wrenched his horse around and aimed the animal at Quigley. Just in time he dived to one side and turned to shoot again at the man – then paused, as the rider, realizing how close he was to the edge of the canyon, hauled on the reins.

The horse skidded on the hard rock surface as it tried to stop its forward momentum. It teetered on the edge, its hoofs scrabbling for purchase. It almost looked as if it might make it, but then momentum and gravity intervened and horse and rider went over. Quigley heard the horse screaming as it plunged towards that fast-flowing river far below. The man might have been screaming too. Quigley stayed on the ground and fired at the one remaining gunman. He threw up his hands.

'Don't shoot,' he yelled, 'I give up.'

Then he stopped yelling as a rifle bullet took out the back of his head. He pitched forwards and fell from the saddle, spilling blood and brains on to the hard ground. Suddenly it was all over. Except for the horses milling around, all the members of the murder gang were sprawled amidst the rocks with bloody wounds – testimony to the accurate shooting of Quigley and his rescuer.

He stayed where he was, the acrid mixture of blood and gunsmoke bitter in his nostrils. Over the neighing of dead riders' horses he heard the clatter of hoofbeats and turned his attention to the rider approaching.

'You all right, Quigley?' Murray called.

Slowly Quigley stood. 'Knocked about a mite, but alive.'

He surveyed the scene of the gunfight – the execution gang sprawled about in various attitudes of death. The dead men's horses had calmed down somewhat, but the smell of cordite and blood was making them skittish.

'I thought I told you to head for Templeton,' he chided.

'You know I never was one to follow orders. I didn't think much to your plan, so I hung around in case I was needed.' Murray dismounted even as he spoke. 'I guess I was proved right.'

Quigley gripped his friend's hand.

'Thanks Murray. That's another steak I owe you when this is over.'

'Aw hell, that's what friends are for. What about this lot here? What are we going to do about them?'

'I guess they ain't going anywhere soon. We'll have to find some place to hole up until we figure out our next move. We're dealing with a snake – a shrewd, callous and vicious hellion. If we are to best him we need to be every bit as cunning and merciless as he is.'

26

Huston McRae was out at the corrals supervising a fresh delivery of horses. They were replacement mounts for the cowboys that rode herd on his vast cattle empire. The ranch boss had a hands-on approach to his cattle rearing and the men appreciated that. Though they feared him they also respected him.

The wranglers who had delivered the stock were tending to their own mounts and waiting for McRae's assessment. Finished his inspection the ranch boss told the drovers to come up to the house to complete the payment details. During this process one of Slater's deputies arrived from Slimwater and waited for the rancher to conclude his business. At last McRae called him inside.

'Sheriff Slater sent me to tell you two men arrived in town asking for you. Names of Todd Sloane and Blane Golay.'

'OK,' McRae said, 'go back to town. Tell Slater to keep those two under wraps until I get there.'

After the deputy departed McRae sent for his straw-boss. Stanley Hagerman was a tall lean man who moved with the lithe gliding movement that might be reminiscent of the way a snake moves. Even his eyes had a stony cold-ness. No one would ever dare make the snake suggestion to his face. His reputation was such he could silence a recalcitrant cowboy with one look from those cold eyes.

'Sloane and Golay are in town,' McRae said. 'I need to

go in there and pay them for that job they did in Idlereach. I'll need you with me.'

'Sure.'

'Are the boys back from Mammoth Heights yet?'

'Don't expect them for a while. Knowing Birney and Harden as well as I do, my guess is they'll want to make Quigley's death a mite painful and prolonged. They'll take their time over killing him.'

'Yeah, as long as they make sure no one ever finds the body. Quigley has to vanish off the face of the earth. As far as anybody knows he just upped and rode away.'

'They're good men. They'll do the job proper.' Hagerman paused a moment looking speculatively at his boss. 'Mr McRae, I been thinking about them two fellas, Sloane and Golay. It was me as hired them for that Barker killing, and I know them well. We used to ride together. Sloane has a loose mouth. What if he gets drunk some time and boasts about that killing over in Idlereach? Maybe let's slip who gave them the contract. I don't want to be in no frame over that. Quigley told Slater he wired some judge to send marshals to help him take over the law office here. If they ever turn up and get to digging around, who knows what they might come up with?'

McRae leaned back in his chair. 'Take a seat,' he said. 'You want a cigar?'

'Nah, I prefer my own.'

Hagerman took out the makings and began the process of rolling a cigarette. McRae reached for a cigar and held it in hand while he mulled over what his straw boss had said.

'Hang dang it, you're right,' the ranch boss said at last. 'This whole business has been a mess ever since my brother tangled with Peter Barker. Who'd have guessed a two-bit sheriff from Idlereach would come all the way over here to track down a killing that happened on his own patch. How'd he make the connection in the first place?'

'We'll never know now. He'll take his secret to a rocky grave in Mammoth Heights. One other thing, there was another fella with him. Big fella as whipped some of our boys at the livery stable. Maybe he needs taking care of besides.'

McRae shook his head in exasperation, then fired up his cigar.

'One problem at a time. Get a few of the boys together and we'll ride into Slimwater. Virgil and Justin are due in on the stage. We'll meet up with them and take care of Sloane and Golay at the same time. Then we can have a night of fun. We'll make it a double celebration – my brother and my son's homecoming, and the winding up of the Quigley affair. You and the boys can have free drinks all night.'

'Sure thing, boss.' Hagerman stood. 'I'll be glad when these shenanigans are over. I was organizing a head count of stock with a view to putting together a cattle drive. We could do with selling off a batch of steers. Then this Quigley business broke. The schedule is all torn to shreds what with having to pull men off the range to hunt for the son of a bitch. And then there's the fellas his partner jumped at the livery and put in the sick bay. They are well out of the action. I don't know when they'll be fit for work again.'

'Huh! Pay them off. They're a pack of useless galoots. Ain't got no room for fellas as let themselves be jumped by one man. They're just dead wood. We can always hire more when this business is finished. Things will be back to normal after today.'

Hagerman left the house and strode out to the corral where cowboys were sorting out the newly arrived horses. Before being set to work out on the range, the ponies had to be rested and fed and watered. Bronco busters would

then trial them to find out which were saddle broke and
fit for work. Within a few days they would be part of the
Circle M remuda. The straw boss selected five men from
the cowboys working on the herd. Eli Menagh – red-
haired with a round face and black button eyes;
Chistopher Brevan – blond-haired and of lanky build with
a dour countenance; Phesley Meissner – balding and soft-
bellied but tough as a buffalo; Edmon McMinn –
soft-bellied also, but with small, mean eyes and a permanent scowl; and finally Charlie Farnham, blue eyed with
bushy sideburns and large build. All five men were killers,
recruited by Hagerman for just those qualities.

They had ridden with the straw boss in the past when
they operated outside the law. Now they were operating as
McRae's enforcers. Better pay than when they robbed
banks and stagecoaches. Now they would tag along with
Hagerman and McRae as a guarantee that the two men
would be taken care of. They would kill their former com-
rades without compunction or remorse. Killing was
something they all enjoyed.

'Be ready to ride,' Hagerman told them. 'We have to
take care of a couple of loose-mouthed rannies. Boss says
as there will be free drinks to celebrate.'

'Who are we gunning for?' asked Charlie Farnham.

'Couple of old comrades-in-arms, Todd Sloane and
Blane Goley.'

'They here! I heard they were jailed after a shootout.'

'Don't figure how they did it, but they're here now in
Slimwater. Mr McRae has a long reach. I guess he might
have had something to do with their escape.'

27

Quigley and Murray rode away from the carnage in Mammoth Heights pondering their next move and very aware they were pitted against a powerful and ruthless cattle baron. He had surrounded himself with killers, and Quigley knew that these men would now be gunning for him and Murray. He had no doubt, if he were to trawl through wanted notices, he would come across the faces of murderers and bandits who were now in the employ of McRae.

'I think we got to go back to our original plan,' Quigley said at last. 'We go into Slimwater, only instead of holing up in the jail, we stay loose and pick off McRae's people as and when they come for us. First we take out Slater and his deputies. I already took care of two of them. Then we run for the hills. Anyone as comes after us we ambush. We make raids on them out on the trail so they are afraid to leave the ranch except in gangs. That way we can hold out until Judge Updegrove sends help.'

'If he ever does? What if the judge has a heart attack and dies and nobody comes to help? Or if someone assassinates him? What then?'

'What if, what if! What if we rode back to Ildlereach and got on with our own lives? Could you live with yourself knowing McRae and his hellions were tearing the American flag to shreds and riding roughshod over the people of Gila County? Would you leave Jemima and Betsy and Noreen to the mercy of such men?'

'Damn it Quigley, you know better than that. All right,

we go into Idlereach and punch a few holes in Slater and his deputies. They'll probably be waiting for us and give us a warm welcome. Hello boys, welcome back. Here's your ticket to boot hill.'

When Quigley did not respond, Murray looked at him. His partner was rising up in the saddle and peering into the distance. He pulled out his glass and took a long look.

'What is it?'

Quigley put his glass back. He turned to Murray, a smirk on his face.

'That's the stage heading into Slimwater. What if we ride the stage in? We get into town and no one sees us until it's too late and we jump them unexpected.'

Murray shrugged.

'Come on, then,' Quigley ordered. 'Look lively. We got a stage to catch.'

They rode hard across country on a path that would intersect with that of the stagecoach. As it was, they had time to spare and were waiting on the road when the coach came upon them. The shotgun guard levelled his piece when he sighted them. It was touch and go whether he thought they were hold-up men. Quigley was holding aloft his sheriff's badge with both hands in the air.

'We're lawmen,' he called. 'Need a ride into Slimwater.'

The driver, thin and sinewy as a lizard, slowed his team. His sidekick was short and stocky with a grizzled beard.

'Why d'you need a ride?' the shotgun shouted. 'You got horses.'

'Throwed a shoe,' Quigley lied. 'Need to get to town and have it redone.'

The coach rolled to a stop.

'OK, hitch them up to the rear. There's room inside. I sure hope you are who you say you are.'

'If I'd meant you harm I'd've shot you off the top of

118

that coach. Keep your gun on me if you like.'

The driver hawked and spat into the road. 'Well, get a move on. I got a schedule to keep.'

Their horses secured to the back rail, Quigley and Murray prepared to climb aboard. The door opened and a gun was thrust from the interior.

'Get rid of those guns and come in slow and careful.'

Quigley stared up at the man behind the gun. Lean and lantern jawed and dressed in a city suit.

'Do you know what you are doing, mister, interfering with the law?'

He heard footsteps as someone walked around the back of the coach. Quigley turned and stared into the smirking face of Virgil McRae. He also was holding a gun, and pointing it at Quigley.

'We meet again, fella,' Virgil said. 'Last time you buffaloed me and I told you I would kill you. I guess now is as good a time as any.'

'Virgil!' the man in the doorway called. 'Not now!'

Virgil leered and kept the gun levelled. Quigley wasn't sure if he couldn't see a hint of madness in the youngster's eyes. He noted the man in the coach lean further out from the doorway in order to deal with the situation.

'Uncle Justin,' Virgil called, 'this is the hellion as bust my teeth so as I had to go to Dry Springs to get that dental work done. So I owe this varmint!'

'Virgil, now is not the time,' Justin called.

'You haven't the guts,' Quigley sneered. 'You'll wet your pants afore you pull that trigger.'

'You think so,' Virgil yelled. The hand that held the gun was shaking.

'You forgot to load the damned thing,' Quigley snorted.

'What. . . .'

The kid couldn't help it. He glanced down at the

weapon. Quigley slammed the coach door in the face of the man leaning out and hurled himself at Virgil. The youngster jerked back to avoid the oncoming lawman and at the same time pulled the trigger. The shot went somewhere over Quigley's shoulder and then he crashed into Virgil, batting away the gun and punching the youngster hard in the chest. With a frightened yell Virgil went down. Quigley towered over him and kicked the gun from his hand. He whirled back to the coach pulling his own weapon, prepared to deal with the man inside. There was no need. Murray was pointing a gun into the coach interior.

'Try for a shot, mister,' he growled, 'and this coach will become your hearse.'

'What the hell's going on?' the guard yelled.

When he saw Virgil on the ground he tried to swing the shotgun around. Quigley pointed his revolver.

'Hold it, fella. I'm a law officer and I'm putting this varmint under arrest. You try to stop me and I have every right to shoot you. So throw down that shotgun.'

'Shoot him, Enoch!' Virgil yelled. 'Shoot the son of a bitch.'

Quigley waited as he saw the guard tense, but then thought it better to obey the man with the gun on him. The shotgun clattered into the well.

'OK mister, you better be sure you know what you are doing. That's Virgil McRae on the ground and his uncle Justin is inside.'

'Justin McRae!' Quigley exclaimed. 'I sure wondered when we would meet up with the other members of the clan.' Quigley stepped back. 'Justin, you throw out that gun or I'll break you nephew's head.'

'No need for any shooting,' Justin called.

He handed his gun out, butt first to Murray.

'On your feet, Virgil,' Quigley ordered. 'We'll all ride

into Slimwater. I reckon I got me a safe passage with two of Huston McRae's family as hostage.'

28

Murray and Quigley climbed inside the coach. There were two other passengers, both male, one with a greying goatee beard and the other younger and clean shaven. They were dressed soberly in duster coats. Both men were packing holstered guns underneath their coats. There was something unsettling about the pair.

'Are you dudes with these men?' Quigley asked, indicating his prisoners.

'What they done?' the older one asked.

'The McRae family are guilty of so many crimes I couldn't list them all. Murder being the most serious charge.'

'What's your name?' the older one asked.

'I'm Sheriff Quigley and this is my deputy, Murray Fishbourne.'

The stranger reached inside his coat and both Quigley and Murray tensed, wondering if the man was about to pull a weapon. Instead he produced a metal badge.

'Marshal Thamon Wattles,' he said. 'And this is Marshal Everet Koder.' Koder nodded briefly at his companion. 'Judge Updegrove sent us. Said as you were in some bother over here and we were to offer you any assistance.'

Quigley tipped his head back and stared up at the roof.

'God bless Judge Leyman Updegrove,' he said ardently. 'You men sure are a welcome addition to the crew.'

'What's going on here anyway? The judge was a mite sparse on details.'

'Gila County is run like a fiefdom by one man, Huston McRae. This is his brother and his son.' Quigley indicated the two men he had taken prisoner. 'He owns the law; he owns about everything and everybody in Gila County. McRae ordered the killing of a man who was running a ranch here and who just happened to be passing through my town, Idlereach, when he was killed. Since then McRae's crew have tried to kill me several times. I aim to go into Slimwater and arrest the sheriff and anyone else connected to the cabal.'

'It's a lie,' interrupted Justin McRae. 'This fella is deluded and paranoid. You fellas are heading for a very painful ordeal if you take his side. We have the law on our side and dozens of gunhands to back us up. You want to live, mister, you stay on this coach when we get to town. It'll take you out of Slimwater and out of danger. You take sides in this and you'll end up either in jail or dead.'

Quigley backhanded the speaker. 'Shut your mouth!'

Justin glared venomously at his attacker. 'You're a dead man, Quigley. You and that fat piece of lard there with you.' His gaze shifted to the two marshals. 'You take my advice. If you want to go on living, don't get off this coach when it stops in Slimwater.'

'I told you to shut up,' Quigley yelled. 'I'll bend this gun barrel over your head if you don't.'

'Hold on there,' Wattles said. 'Is what he's saying true – about dozens of gunhands and a sheriff along with them? I need to know what the hell we're getting into.'

'Yeah, it's true,' Quigley said testily. 'McRae has the whole territory sewn up. He owns everyone and everything.'

'And we're going in there against a mob of gunnies?

Quigley, this don't set right with me. No, the best thing is to wait for the judge to send us reinforcements.' Marshal Wattles jumped to his feet and leaned out the window. 'Stop!' he yelled. 'Stop the coach!'

Quigley pulled on the marshal's coat. 'What are you doing?'

'I'm turning this coach around and going back to the next town. We'll wait there for Judge Updegrove to send more men.'

The stagecoach stopped and the guard dropped to the ground and came to the window.

'What the hell's the matter now?' he growled. 'We can't keep stopping and starting like this.'

'Turn this coach around and head back,' Wattles told him.

'Like hell I will!'

Wattles showed him his badge. 'I'm a United States marshal and I order you to take this coach back.'

'Don't do it, Enoch,' Justin McRae called. 'He ain't got no authority here. Remember who pays your wages.'

Wattles turned from the window. 'Shut the hell up!' he yelled.

But the damage was done. The driver refused point blank to turn around.

'Nothing else for it, Marshal,' Quigley told him. 'You'll have to come along for the ride. Judge Updegrove will more than likely give you a medal when this is all over.'

Wattles' face was red with anger. Then his eyes narrowed as he thought of something. He reached inside his coat and pulled his gun and held it on Quigley.

'What the. . . ?'

'Quigley, I'm commandeering those two horses of yours. I may not be able to turn the coach around, but I can sure ride away from this.' The marshal nodded to his partner. 'Everet, get out and untie those horses.'

The young marshal scrambled from the coach.

'You're a yellow-livered coward, Wattles,' Quigley raged. 'Call yourself a marshal. You ain't even a man!'

'At least I'll be a live one. When we get to the next telegraph, we'll wire the judge for help.'

'Ready, Thamon,' Everet called from outside.

'Bye, sheriff, good luck,' the marshal called as he got off the coach. 'We'll send help as soon as we can.'

The guard peered in the window. 'What now, Mr McRae? You want we should carry on?'

'Sure thing, Enoch. Sooner the better.'

The face disappeared and soon the coach was under way again.

'That worked out well for you, Quigley,' Virgil sneered.

'Shut the hell up,' Quigley snarled, 'afore I shut you up.'

But the youngster was grinning, relishing this turnabout for Quigley. And Quigley was angry. Angry with himself, and angry with the two men who had taken their horses and ridden away.

'I can ask Enoch to stop the coach and let you off,' Justin McRae said. 'It might delay your death a mite. But as soon as we get into town we'll send Sheriff Slater after you. I don't believe two men on foot would be able to outrun a posse.'

'And I could stop this coach and unhitch a couple of horses and ride away from this hell's brew,' Quigley told him.

But that didn't stop Quigley's two prisoners from smirking complacently at the lawmen. The coach rumbled on, taking them closer to Slimwater and whatever fate awaited them there.

*

Once everyone had left the Barrel B, Noreen set about her chores. But even as she worked she could not suppress a nagging feeling that the people in her life were in some kind of trouble. Her mother and her daughter were at school. Quigley and Murray had ridden off on some errand which she guessed would entail an element of danger. In the end her fears and restlessness could not be quelled, and she decided she would ride into Slimwater if only on the pretext of meeting up with her daughter at school.

She saddled up and rode towards town, trying to tell herself not to be so foolish. But after all that had happened she could not shake off the feeling of dread that dogged her.

Slimwater was busy with buggies and carts and wagons, with horsemen adding to the congestion. Even though the town was dominated by one man, it still managed to prosper and grow. Noreen was well aware of the grip McRae had on the town, and knew also that any business that hoped to stay solvent paid a tax to the McRae estate.

She had time on her hands before school ended and decided to do some shopping. She pulled up at the general store and tied up her horse, bracing herself for the ordeal she had to go through each time she visited the place.

Delmar Musgrave and his brother Adrian – crude, big-bellied men – were the proprietors. Ever since the feud with McRae when the Barrel B was blacklisted, the two men took it as a licence to treat her as if she were a saloon girl, with lewd suggestions and invitations to come out back to pay for the goods she bought.

Shaking and angry she left the store, jamming her purchases into the saddlebags. She paused to watch the stage pull in, then sucked in her breath as Justin McRae stepped down, followed by his nephew Virgil. To add to her shock at seeing the man who had been the cause of the feud between her husband and the McRaes, Quigley also got off the stage, and was joined by Murray. Noreen stayed by her tethered horse and watched.

29

Quigley kept a close eye on his prisoners as he stepped down from the stage, his hands never far from his holstered Colts. Murray climbed down and stood by, equally watchful.

'You're going to regret this, fella,' Justin said. 'My brother will kill you as he would a rat in his barn.'

'The only rats I know are the ones with the surname McRae,' Quigley replied. 'Now get a move on. I'm taking you to jail.'

There was a movement from the coach and Quigley looked up. The guard had his shotgun lined up on Quigley, while beside him the driver had a revolver aimed at Murray.

'What the hell's going on?' Quigley yelled. 'You're breaking the law, throwing down on two law officers.'

'Mister, I work for Mr McRae. He pays me to deliver this coach and passengers safely. And that's what I aim to do. So, just you back off there and shed those guns. I answer to Mr McRae, not some two-bit hustler.'

'Good work, Enoch,' Virgil called. 'You'll get a bonus

for this day's work. Do like he says and hand over those Colts.'

Quigley stared up at the men on the coach. Only a few yards separated them. If the guard let fly with that shotgun, Quigley would be splattered all over the street.

'Damn you,' he swore.

'Unbuckle your gunbelts and let them drop in the dirt,' Justin ordered. 'Then we can all go down the jail and put you two away safe.' He sniggered. 'That is until we can organize a hanging in your honour.'

With some agitation, Noreen watched the stand-off across the street. She could see exactly what was happening and that Quigley and Murray were in trouble. Noreen reached out and pulled her rifle from the saddle scabbard. Her insides were quivering as she stepped into the roadway, her weapon aimed at the men atop the coach.

'Hold up there,' she called. 'What's going on here?'

Just as Noreen intervened there was a shout from further up the street. All heads turned to look. Hagerman, with three other gunmen, were striding towards them. He had been sent by McRae to bring his son and brother back to the Red Nugget where he was waiting to celebrate the family reunion.

'Noreen. . . !' Quigley yelled.

The warning came too late. A brawny pair of arms closed around Noreen and she was hauled backwards.

'I got the Barker woman,' Delmar Musgrave yelled out.

Noreen was struggling in vain in the big man's embrace. His brother reached out and wrenched the rifle from Noreen's hands. He held up the weapon.

'I reckon she was figuring to shoot you, Mr McRae,' he yelled.

Across the street Quigley saw Noreen struggling in the grip of the storekeeper. The man's brother put Noreen's rifle to her head.

'You want me to blow her brains out, Mr McRae?'

'Hold her there,' McRae called. 'If these fellas don't give up their guns then put a bullet in her. Somewhere it'll hurt, but not kill her.'

And then Quigley's options closed as Hagerman and his gunnies reached them with drawn guns.

'What'll it be, Quigley?' Hagerman called. 'You're in a bind. You ain't got a chance.'

Quigley's shoulders slumped. Hagerman was right. The odds of any of them surviving were close to nil. With the two men on the coach ready to pour lead down on them and the four gunmen just arrived, he and Murray wouldn't stand a chance. They would be cut to pieces before they could get off a shot. And then there was Noreen, held hostage across the street.

'OK,' he growled. 'I'll come with you. Let Mrs Barker go. She's an innocent party in all this.'

'Yeah, as soon as you throw your irons down, then she can go free.'

Quigley looked at Murray. For answer the big man unbuckled his gunbelt and allowed the rig to fall to the dirt. Quigley had no option but to do the same.

'Yippee!' Virgil yelled. 'Shoot the son of a bitch.'

'No,' Hagerman called. 'That's for the boss to decide. We take them to Mr McRae. He'll deal with them.'

But Virgil was not to be denied. He stepped towards Quigley and swung a punch. Quigley swayed back, grabbed the youngster's arm and slammed him against the side of the coach. Virgil yelped as his nose was pulped.

'Enough,' Justin yelled. 'Back off, Quigley.'

'Keep your puppy dog on a leash, then,' Quigley snarled.

Justin grabbed his nephew and pulled him away.

'You'll get your chance to hurt him, Virgil. Let's go and see your pa. We'll have a drink and we can all enjoy watching them hang.'

Cursing and struggling Virgil was hauled back.

'Walk up the street,' Hagerman instructed Quigley, gesturing with his gun. 'How the hell did you end up back here? I sent some good men to make sure you stayed up in the hills permanent.'

'We agreed to swop places. You won't be seeing any of those hellhounds anytime soon.'

'Damn you! Now get moving. Head on down to the Red Nugget. I guess we could all do with a drink. You men on the coach climb down and help us keep these fellas covered. If they managed to bushwhack the men I sent up into Mammoth Heights they are capable of anything. I want every man's fingers on triggers. They make any false moves, just shoot and keep on shooting. You there with the shotgun, keep it on Quigley. I'm sure Mr McRae won't be too concerned if he arrives with a few holes in his hide.'

The gunmen spread out across the street with weapons trained on the captives. Quigley looked across at Noreen. The big storekeeper still held her while his brother kept the rifle against her head.

'Let her go,' he yelled.

'What you say, Mr McRae?' the storekeeper called. 'You want her let go?'

'Do what the hell you like,' Hagerman snarled. 'You snagged her, so you deal with her.'

'Son of a bitch!' Quigley yelled. 'Leave her be. You promised.'

Hagerman fired a shot into the dirt in front of Quigley.

'Just start walking afore I put a bullet in your belly,' he snarled. 'She's our guarantee you'll behave.'

Quigley glanced down at his guns lying in the dirt. He was tempted to grab a weapon and take his chances.

'Don't let them take you, Quigley,' Noreen shouted, as if she read his thoughts.

A beefy hand clamped across her mouth. They stared at each other across those few yards that separated them. Noreen's eyes blazed defiance, her expression urging him not to give in. Quigley marvelled at her spirit. More than anything else he wanted to know she would be safe. It didn't matter about him, but it mattered what happened to Noreen.

Quigley did not know the calibre of the men who held her captive, whether or not they were capable of shooting an innocent woman. But he knew he could not take that chance. He could not allow himself to be the instrument of her being hurt. With an effort Quigley dropped his eyes, breaking the contact with Noreen.

'Just make sure she ain't harmed,' he said.

'Do as you're told then,' Hagerman growled.

Quigley turned and shuffled along the street with Murray beside him. He had no other option. There was nowhere else to go.

30

Betsy pulled the buggy to a stop, peering along the street at the group of people clustered around the stage depot. She could see there was something amiss, and didn't want to drive into a possible fracas. Jemima and her pal Joanna were in the seat beside her, chatting. The girls looked up when the buckboard stopped. As Betsy began to make out details, a cold sense of dread grew within her. She saw Hagerman and his sidekicks holding guns on Quigley and Murray. Saw the two McRaes. Saw her daughter being manhandled by the storekeepers.

'What's Mr Musgrave doing with Ma?' Jemima cried out. 'He's hurting her!'

She stood as if to shout, and quickly Betsy hushed her.

'Wait, child, wait until we see what's going on here.'

'But Momma. . .' wailed Jemima.

Betsy put her arm around her. 'Shush. Just let's wait to see what is happening.'

Jemima sat, her hand across her mouth, eyes wide and staring. They watched as Quigley and Murray were escorted down the street at gunpoint. Noreen was struggling against the Musgrave brothers. They were conferring and evidently came to some conclusion, because they dragged Noreen across the street and into the store.

Betsy sat frozen in the buggy, staring at the now empty street. A few curious people stood on the boardwalks watching the drama, but no one interfered. Betsy turned to the children.

'Jemima, I want you to be brave.' She handed over the traces to the girl. 'I want you to drive to Joanna's house and stay there with her. In a little while Mama and me will come by for you. Will you do that for me?'

'What are you going to do?' Jemima whimpered.

'I am going to collect your mother from the store and maybe do some shopping and then we will come for you.'

'I'm scared, Grandma.'

'I know, darling. But I know, too, that you are the bravest little girl.'

131

Betsy climbed down from the buggy. She reached in the back and pulled out her rifle.

'Remember what I told you. We'll come and fetch you soon.'

Jemima nodded dumbly, flicked the reins to get the horse started. Betsy watched it go, then turned and marched towards the store. When she tried to enter she found the door was locked. For a moment she hesitated, then jacked a shell into the chamber and shot the lock to pieces and kicked the door open. Jacked another shell and stepped inside. The room was empty of people. She marched towards the rear of the store, and a head appeared from behind the counter.

'What the hell are you doing?' Delmar Musgrave shouted. 'Can't you see we're closed?'

Betsy next shot smashed a jar of molasses on a shelf behind the counter. The wild-eyed head of Adrian popped up beside that of his brother. Behind them the gooey mess dripped from the smashed jar.

'Get the hell out here where I can see you,' snarled Betsy. 'Else you'll have a third eye in that thick skull of yours. What have you done with my daughter?'

There was a sudden flurry of movement behind the counter and Noreen stood up. She was hatless, with her hair awry and her blouse torn. She also had a bloody nose and a bruised eye. Her hesitation was only momentary as her eyes met those of Betsy.

Noreen snatched up a steel coffee grinder and slammed it against the storekeeper's head. With a yell he disappeared from view. His brother was staring open mouthed at Noreen, then the improvised weapon swept round and slammed his mouth closed. He too disappeared from view. Noreen looked wildly around her. Then she snatched a bottle from the row behind her. There came the sound of breaking glass as she smashed it on someone's head.

'Goddamn it!' Delmar yelled and a thick pair of hands reached up to grapple with Noreen. She jammed the broken neck of the bottle into the beefy arm and the owner shrieked. The arm disappeared out of sight and its owner moaned piteously. Betsy strode over and looked down at the brothers cowering on the floor.

'Come out of there, Noreen. They've had enough.'

Noreen was looking around for something and then she spotted it. She strode over and grabbed up her rifle, tossed aside when the brothers dragged her into the store. Holding the weapon by the barrel, she looked around wildly and then began smashing bottles and jars, clearing shelves in a frenzy of anger. Betsy hesitated only momentarily, then she too lent a hand.

Pots and pans and ceramic jars exploded in an orgy of destruction as the two women give vent to their anger. Shelves were swept empty. Displays were demolished. Demijohns smashed to shards. Clothing flung in disarray into the myriad substances flowing from the shattered containers. And while their store was being devastated Delmar and his brother Adrien cowered on the floor, too terrified to confront the furies. As their passion dissipated Noreen paused, breathing heavily, gazing around her at the devastation.

'Feeling better, honey?' Betsy asked.

'I'd feel a lot better when I put a bullet in these two brutes,' Noreen panted.

She reversed the weapon and pointed the barrel at the terrified men. They cowered back whimpering, putting hands over their heads as if to ward off the bullets they were convinced were about to blast holes in their well-fleshed bodies.

'Don't, Noreen. They ain't worth it.'

Slowly Noreen lowered the weapon. She looked up sharply as a thought struck her.

'Quigley and Murray! The McRaes have them. Hagerman took them. They're going to kill them, for sure.'

'Yeah, I saw that. I don't reckon there's much we can do. I really liked those boys.'

'Let's get out there and see what's happening.' Noreen aimed her rifle at the two men crouching behind the counter. 'You poke your heads out that door when we're gone and I'll let some daylight into those fat skulls.'

She stalked to the door.

'Where's your hat?' Betsy asked. 'You can't go out in the street with no hat.'

Noreen put her hand to her head as if she only just realized her headgear was missing. She looked around her but could see no sign of her hat. Her eyes lighted on an overturned rack and she strode over and rummaged about, coming up with a black, low-crowned planter hat. She jammed it on top of her head.

'Well, how do I look?'

'You look like my little girl.'

Noreen stared at her mother and a slow smile spread over her face.

'Thanks, Ma. You did good.'

'Shucks honey, I'm always pulling your ass out of the fire. Ain't that what mothers are for? Your shirt is torn a tad.'

Noreen glanced down at her ripped clothing. For a moment she looked maliciously towards the counter behind which her attackers were hiding and raised her rifle.

'Ain't worth it, Noreen,' Betsy said. 'Just find yourself a

134

shirt – that is, if you can find anything worthwhile amongst all this mess.'

Noreen rummaged about some more and came up with a blue cotton shirt which she pulled on over her own ruined clothing. As she buttoned it she looked with some concern at Betsy.

'What about Quigley? Did you see what happened?'

'I sure did. I guess there ain't nothing anyone can do for them now.'

Noreen looked down at the rifle in her hand. She walked back across the store and ignoring the two men behind the counter, got a gunnysack and filled it with boxes of shells.

'These will make up for the ones you had to fire off to get in here,' she told her mother. 'I want you to collect Jemima and take her back to the ranch.'

'And just what the hell do you think you're going to do in the meantime?'

Noreen strode to the door.

'I owe those boys.'

'By all that's holy,' Betsy said forcefully. 'What can one woman do against a passel of gunmen?'

Mother and daughter stood on the boardwalk staring down the street. Outside the Red Nugget a crowd had gathered and were watching some activity on the street. Not able to see over the heads of the crowd Noreen looked around for a better vantage point and spotted the stagecoach, still parked across from the store. She ran across and climbed on top and stood on the roof. Quigley and Murray were kneeling in the dirt surrounded by McRae's gunnies. Standing on the saloon porch overseeing the activities were the three members of the McRae family.

'What's happening?' Betsy asked.

'Looks like McRae is presiding over a kangaroo court to decide their fate,' Noreen replied.

'No prizes in guessing what that'll be,' Betsy muttered.

31

From his vantage point on the steps of the Red Nugget, Huston McRae glared down at the two men kneeling in the street. He had a cigar wedged between his fingers, and it was this hand he was using to gesture at Quigley and Murray. Both men had their hands tied with rawhide. They stared helplessly at the McRaes, triumphant now they had Quigley and his buddy safely hogtied.

'You've caused me more trouble than anyone I have ever come up against,' Huston McRae growled. 'Well, it stops now.' He glared around at the crowd that had gathered to watch the spectacle. 'These men are killers. I tried to reason with them, but they persevered with their killing. They beat my son so badly I had to send him away for medical treatment. They pistol-whipped Sheriff Slater and murdered two of his deputies. They killed six of my top ranch hands. And now they've tried to hold up the stage. But for Enoch and Irven, along with Justin and my son Virgil, they might have got away with it. I say we can't let such lawlessness go unpunished. What you say, boys? What should we do with these two dangerous killers?'

'String 'em up!' someone yelled.

There was a rumble of agreement from the crowd.

'String 'em up.'

'Hanging's too good for 'em.'

'Murdering scum.'

'Now wait a moment,' McRae said, holding up his hand for silence. 'I guess we ought to let someone speak on behalf of these owlhoots.' He gazed around at the faces in the crowd. 'Who'd like to play devil's advocate? Someone to put the case for these murderers so as anyone can't say as we didn't act fairly by them?'

There was some muttering from the crowd, but nobody took up the challenge.

'No one, huh! I guess that makes me mighty proud of my fellow countrymen. When this business is finished there'll be free drinks all round.' McRae returned his attention back to the captives. 'You fellas anything to say afore the good people of Slimwater hang you for your many crimes?'

'Some day, justice will catch up with you,' Quigley growled. 'No man can go on flouting the law as you do. Maybe I won't be around to see it, but it surely is bound to come.'

'A false witness shall not go unpunished, and he that committeth foul deeds shall face the wrath of the Lord,' Murray voice boomed out.

'I like a god-fearing man,' McRae said affably, 'I guess you'll be able to put your case to the good Lord himself shortly. Sheriff Slater, seeing as you are the law around here, would you do the honours, and escort these gents to a suitable place for a hanging?'

Slater stepped forward a smirk on his face. 'It'll be my pleasure, Mr McRae.'

'The hanging tree,' a man in the crowd shouted. 'Over by the livery.'

'Sure thing,' another called. 'I remember when they hanged Mitchel Kittson for cattle rustling. It sure was a sight to see. Must 'a kicked for a good half hour.'

There was a lot of chatter from the crowd as the idea took fire.

'Come on. Let's do it.'

'Let's hang the murdering scum.'

The captives were kicked to their feet. Sheriff Slater smirked at Quigley.

'I told you how this would end,' he sneered. 'I'm going to enjoy seeing you swing on the end of that rope.'

He gave his victim a vicious shove. Quigley staggered and almost fell. The noise from the crowd swelled. Suddenly everyone was surging forward, calling out insults and threats.

With Slater and his deputies taking turns to hassle them, the prisoners had a hard time keeping on their feet. Following at a discreet distance walked the McRae family. The two older men looking smugly satisfied, while Virgil could hardly restrain himself.

'Can I haul on the rope, Pa?' he asked excitedly. 'I owe that son of a bitch.'

'Yeah, you can pull on the rope, son,' he was told.

'When I hang that son of a bitch, I reckon it'll be the best day of my life.'

His pa laughed out loud. 'That's my boy – a chip off the old block. It makes me proud to see you so eager to mete out justice to those who challenge the McRae name. It'll make my day too, when I see you hauling on that rope and that son of a bitch dangling in the air.'

The mob surged past the livery where Murray had dished out a beating to McRae's thugs and subsequently recovered the stolen buggy. A few hundred yards further on stood a group of pine trees.

'Bring a rope!' someone shouted.

A couple of men went in the livery and emerged with

the man Murray had half drowned when trying to obtain information about the stolen buggy. Between them they were carrying the ropes.

'That's the varmint as near drowned me,' he yelled. 'Deserves to be whupped afore you hang him!'

The mob surged on towards the site of the hanging. There was some delay while Slater and his deputies discussed how to go about the execution.

'We need to put 'em on a horse.'

'Hell, no. Just haul on the rope. We got plenty here as will be willing to do it.'

'Yeah, put the rope around their necks and hoist 'em on high.'

'Get the ropes up.'

There was some delay while the ropes were reeled out and nooses were fashioned. People were crowding around and the deputies had to push them back. The branches to be used for gallows were more than forty feet up the trunk of the tree and the deputies were finding it difficult to get the ropes in position.

'Hell, give us some room to work here.'

'Let Mr McRae in. He'll want a ringside seat.'

'We're almost ready, Mr McRae. Just got to get these ropes in place.'

They managed to sling one of the ropes to a great cheer from the onlookers. In another few minutes the second rope was in position accompanied by another round of applause.

'You anything to say afore we string you up?' Sheriff Slater asked the prisoners, as he fitted the nooses around their necks.

'This is murder,' Quigley said through gritted teeth. 'Some day you'll answer for this crime. Then you'll find yourself in the same position as us today. Think on that.'

Slater punched Quigley in the face and he staggered back.

'That's for that crack on the head you gave me,' Slater told him. 'You killed my deputies. Now you're paying the penalty for your crimes.'

Virgil McRae stepped up. 'I want to be the one to haul them into the air,' he told the sheriff.

'Sure thing, Virgil. I want two men on each rope.'

The volunteers stepped forward and grasped the ropes. A sudden silence fell on the crowd.

'Take them up, boys,' the sheriff yelled.

The ropes tautened and Quigley's feet left the ground as he was hauled into the air. The noose tightened around his neck and he tensed his muscles in an effort to counteract the choking.

He was rotating – one moment seeing the crowd below him and the next moment the tree trunk. Murray was turning beside him also. For a brief moment their eyes met and then they spun away again. Spinning. The tree. Murray. The sky. That terrible choking noose around his neck.

32

There was a rumble back in the street, barely noticeable at first. The mob was so taken up with the sight of the two men dangling in the air no one took much notice of the noise. The reverberations grew more pronounced. A few men glanced towards the town, wondering. The noise became clearer. A vehicle being driven at speed. The crack of a whip, the thudding of hoofs, the rumble of wheels. Into sight swung the source of the disturbance. Men turned and gawped. The stagecoach came on at speed. The sight was so odd no one could make sense of it. The stagecoach thundering towards the scene of the lynching.

'Runaway!' someone yelled.

'Watch out!'

And then the vehicle was on them, scattering onlookers. Some men did not make it. The panicked horses crashed into them, bowling men left, right and centre. The driver hauling on the reins as if trying to control the stampeding horses. The brake jammed on – the wheels locked and skidding the last few yards and the coach jerking to a halt by the hanging tree.

Someone on top grabbing Quigley – a knife blade flashing in the sun. Murray pulled over on top of the coach to come crashing down beside Quigley. The whip curling out over the backs of the horses, the driver screaming at them. The horses heaving in the traces pulling the coach again. The coach drawing away, leaving a pair of cut ropes swinging in the breeze. The shaken mob not quite able to take in what had happened, staring after the coach in bewilderment.

Slowly the noise of the wildly driven stagecoach receded into the distance, to be replaced by the cries of the injured. Men came active again. Curses and calls for action. Huston McRae and his straw boss Hagerman trying to reassert control. Suddenly McRae gave a cry. He walked towards a form huddled beneath the hanging tree. Slowly he knelt and turned the body over, and gave vent to a wail of despair.

'My boy, my boy!'

The side of Virgil's face was caved in where it had been hit by a coach wheel. Blood oozed from the terrible wound, the bones laid bare showing jaws and teeth. Incredibly the body twitched and the one good eye opened. The mouth worked as if the wounded youth was trying to say something.

'My boy . . .' McRae wept. 'My boy. . . .'

'Fetch the sawbones,' someone was yelling.

All around the cries of anger rose louder and louder. Intent on lynching the two men, now the mob was bewildered and shocked and trying to make sense of the happenings.

Stanley Hagerman stood near McRae, his cold eyes watching dispassionately as his boss gave vent to his grief. Sheriff Slater approached, wild-eyed and hatless with dust on his clothing.

'Damn blasted coach knocked me over,' he exclaimed. 'Broke Sidney Harvey's leg. . . .'

The sheriff trailed off as he saw McRae and the person he was holding.

'Jeez!' The sheriff quickly recovered. 'Some men here, we need someone to take Virgil to the sawbones.'

McRae watched helplessly as his son was picked up and carried away. He stood, dusting at his trousers where he had been kneeling. At length he turned cold eyes on the sheriff.

'Get a posse organized and get after that stagecoach. Did anyone see who was driving it?'

'There's folk as is saying it was the Barker women on the coach,' Slater told him.

'You get after it now. Don't come back without them.' McRae paused. Men were crowding around watching. McRae raised his voice. 'A thousand dollars for each of the people on that coach. Dead or alive. Just bring them back. Dead or alive.'

'Sure boss, right away,' Slater vowed. 'We'll catch them.

Don't worry about that.'

'A thousand dollars!' someone shouted. 'A thousand dollar reward for those killers.'

Slater immediately began recruiting men for the posse. He did not have any bother making up the numbers. Once it became known about the reward, everyone who had a horse wanted in on it. It took a while to organize, but eventually a body of horsemen numbering more than fifty gathered outside the sheriff's office. Slater addressed the crowd, that only an hour or so beforehand had been a lynch mob and now were formed into a posse.

'OK, men, you know what has happened. Those two killers have escaped justice for now. And we know who helped them escape – Noreen Barker and her ma, Betsy Gallagher. Mr McRae has put a thousand dollar reward on each of them. That is on all four of them. That's four thousand dollars for the benefit of those of you who can't count.' This feeble jest brought a low murmur from the assembled horsemen. 'Also Mr McRae ain't bothered how we bring 'em in.' He paused for effect. 'Dead or alive is what he said. So if any man can't abide the thought of shooting a female, I guess he'd better go on back home. I want no candy-assed backsliders on this trip.' The sheriff glared at the horsemen as if daring someone to contradict him. No one did. 'We'll go by the Red Nugget, let Mr McRae know we're on our way.'

A deputy held his horse while Slater mounted and led the way along the street, the posse falling in behind, making up a formidable force. Slater stopped outside the saloon and climbed down. He went inside and after a few minutes came back out again.

'Mr McRae says his offer of free drinks still stands,' he called. 'So the sooner we catch those sidewinders the sooner we'll be back here to celebrate.'

A cheer went up from the posse. Sheriff Slater climbed back on his mount and waved his arm in the air.

'Forward men,' he yelled. 'Remember, dead or alive. And a thousand dollars riding on their heads.'

The posse rode out of Slimwater trailing a cloud of dust, every rider intent on getting a slice of that reward money.

33

'Pull in behind the schoolhouse,' Betsy yelled in Noreen's ear.

She was lying on the coach roof clinging on to the guardrail. Beside her lay Quigley and Murray, now recovered enough to hang on to the rail as well. Noreen did as she was told and eased the vehicle around in a curve that took her towards the school. As she hauled on the reins and pulled the brake handle the coach came to a halt behind the school building. She turned to help Betsy with the two rescued men.

'Come on you fellas, look lively,' Betsy chided.

Lively was certainly not the word for Quigley or Murray. They allowed themselves to be chivvied from the stage. Betsy pointed to a lean-to. Luckily there was no one around to observe them. It seemed everyone had gone up town to view the lynching.

'In there.'

Noreen guided the men inside while Betsy unloaded guns and ammunition from the interior of the coach. She

144

drove the coach back on the main trail, climbed down and took up the whip and began lashing the unfortunate animals.

'Hip, hip, hip,' she yelled. 'Get along there.'

Already nervy from the wild drive into the mob, the horses neighed shrilly and took off. Betsy stood in the road and watched to make sure they kept running.

'Run, my beauties. Don't stop running until you cross the state boundary.'

She turned and threaded her way through the back alleys to rejoin her companions. Inside the lean-to, Quigley and his partner were recovered enough to thank their rescuers.

'We were dead meat,' Quigley said hoarsely, massaging his throat, 'then you come along.'

'I thought you were heavenly angels come to escort me to the happy hunting grounds,' Murray said in a whispery husky voice. 'Thank you! We can never repay you for this deed you done today.'

'Shucks,' Betsy said. 'You're the only good men for miles around. We couldn't not rescue you.'

At that point the door was thrust open and a woman's face appeared in the opening.

'What on earth is going on here?'

There was a moment of silence as they stared at Sophronia Wineteer, the schoolteacher and wife of the preacher. She slowly stepped inside.

'Sophronia,' Betsy began and stumbled to a halt.

'These are the men they were going to hang,' Sophronia said. 'I heard about it. It was to be a lynching. I never thought I would ever see that sort of behaviour in my own town. It makes me ashamed to be part of this community.'

'Ma'am, we're no criminals,' Quigley said. 'I'm Sheriff

Quigley from Idlereach where Mrs Barker's husband Peter was murdered. I arrested the men who killed him and came here to bring the sad news to Peter's family. Since arriving here I found out his death was orchestrated from Slimwater by the McRae family. I tried to arrest Huston McRae . . .' He shrugged and lifted his arms. 'That is the reason for the lynching. He had to silence me.'

Sophronia regarded him for a moment. 'What do you intend to do now?'

The sound of horses on the move interrupted her. She held up her hand.

'Stay here. I'll try and find out what's happening.' Then she was gone.

'What do you think?' Quigley asked. 'Will she give us away?'

'Sophronia is a good woman.' Betsy said. 'She won't betray us. Best we wait here until she tells us different.'

Quigley went across to the small pile of weapons Betsy had rescued from the coach.

'I see you got our guns back.'

He picked up his gunbelt and buckled it around his waist. Murray came over for his.

'We found them dumped by the stagecoach depot.'

'Whatever happens now, at least we can fight back,' Quigley said. He paused. 'You realize you ain't safe around here anymore. After what you've done, McRae will hound you out of your home. I reckon we brought a lot of trouble on your heads.'

'Trouble,' Noreen snorted. 'McRae's the one as brought trouble on our heads. He murdered Peter and he's tried to murder you. All you did was expose the rotting carcass that is Slimwater. But you're right. None of us is safe after this day's work.'

In a while Sophronia returned.

146

'They've sent a posse after you. Mr McRae has offered a thousand dollars reward. I was almost tempted myself. That sort of money would build a mighty fine school-house.' She smiled. 'But that would be Judas money. I've harnessed up the church buckboard. You take it and get as far away as possible. With no one about you should get through the town without anyone noticing you.'

'Sophronia.' Noreen stepped forward. 'This might well put you in danger.'

The schoolteacher took Noreen's hands in hers.

'The good Lord will look after me as I'm sure he will look after you,' she told her. 'And let us not be weary in well doing: for in due season we shall reap our reward if we faint not.' She glanced around the room. 'God bless you all and keep you safe. I only wish I could do more.'

'You have saved our lives,' Murray said gallantly. 'This is what the Lord asks of you; only this: to act justly, to love tenderly and to walk humbly with your brethren. You, ma'am, are an example of the good Christian woman.'

'Hush now and go. I'm only doing what any right think-ing person would do.'

The buckboard was parked by the side of the school-house. Betsy opted to drive and Murray sat up beside her. Quigley and Noreen sat in the rear. No one said anything, but they were all very much aware that if they were spotted, fireworks would erupt.

'Gee up!' Betsy called and got the buggy moving for-wards.

They had no option but to travel through the town, for there was one member of the family still to be picked up. Jemima would be waiting for them at her friend's house.

34

The atmosphere in the Red Nugget Saloon was sombre – Huston McRae brooding on the injuries sustained by his son, now being cared for at the doctor's surgery. He was drinking steadily, as was his brother Justin.

Stanley Hagerman was staying sober. However, he was plying drink on the two men marked for killing – Todd Sloane and Blane Golay. They were two dangerous gunnies, but Hagerman had no qualms about dealing with them when the time came for their execution. After all, he would have five gunslingers at his back when the time came to carry out McRae's orders.

'Hell,' Todd Sloane groused, 'we should have gone with that posse. I'd've liked to be the one to put a bullet in Quigley.'

'Yeah,' agreed his partner Blane Golay, 'we sure as hell owe that maverick. How the hell they allowed him to get away beats me. Had him hogtied and the noose in place and he vamooses in a danged stagecoach.'

'The posse will run him down,' Hagerman told them. 'There's fifty to sixty men hankering on getting their hands on that reward. They'll bring Quigley back tied across his horse.'

'Talking about reward, McRae promised us a bonus when we took care of that Barker fella. He still owes us that.'

'You'll get paid,' Hagerman told him. 'Mr McRae is a man of his word. Didn't he spring you from that jail?'

'Hell, we'd've got out without his help. Ain't a jail built as can hold Todd Sloane.'

'Maybe, but you're here now, and we'll take care of you. So drink up. It's all on Mr McRae.'

'Maybe we should go somewhere with a bit more life,' Golay suggested. 'This place is like a morgue.'

Hagerman wandered over to where McRae and his brother were drinking, talking in low voices. Huston McRae looked up as his straw boss approached.

'Those rannies are getting restless,' Hagerman told him. 'They're itching to move on.'

'Maybe it's time to give them what they're asking for. Finish that one piece of business afore the posse comes back. The fewer witnesses the better.'

'Sure thing, Mr McRae. I'll take care of it.'

Hagerman sauntered back to the gunmen.

'Mr McRae says as we can take you out for a good time. We'll go down the Honey Bear. The gals there claim to be the best in the west.'

Sloane stood up from the table and swayed slightly.

'Hell, damn it, that's more like it. You've kept us closed up here tighter than a banker's wallet. Let's go and have some fun.'

'Sure thing,' Golay enjoined, clambering to his feet. 'Let's do it.'

Hagerman allowed the two killers to lead the way. He signalled to his crew and the five gunmen fell in behind as they headed for the door.

'Go steady through the town,' Quigley instructed Betsy. 'We're just a party of law-abiding citizens heading for home. Act natural. We'll be all right.'

Ahead of them a man came out of the Red Nugget. Quigley had his hat pulled down low in an attempt at keeping his face hidden in the unlikely event someone might recognize him. He had one of his Colts in his hand. In the seat facing him Noreen sat pale and nervous, her rifle resting on her lap.

More men spilled out of the saloon. It was too late to make a detour. Betsy kept straight on, hoping there was no one in the crowd that would know her. Murray slipped his hand on to the butt of his revolver. Betsy's rifle was leaning in the well, within reach if needed.

'Howdy folks,' Todd Sloane called as he saw the buggy approach. 'Nice evening for a bit of fun. Maybe you ladies would like to join us.'

Sloane leered drunkenly up at Betsy. Betsy shook her head.

'Not tonight, cowboy. I already got a date.'

Sloane grabbed at the bridle as the horse drew level.

'Maybe I ain't good enough for you?' he snarled, suddenly turning ugly.

'Let it go, Todd,' Hagerman called. He glanced at the man sitting on top with Betsy. 'Son of a bitch,' he yelled, 'that's him.'

Hagerman was fast. His gun was out of the holster almost before he finished shouting. Quigley had been keeping low, hoping they might bluff their way out of this situation, but he was also ready with his own weapon. But before he could shoot, Hagerman got off a shot at Murray, hitting him in the side. Murray grunted but dragged out his own weapon.

Quigley fired at the straw boss, hitting him in the shoulder. Hagerman staggered back, but returned fire, hitting the side of the buckboard. Sloane was fumbling for his own weapon when Murray shot him in the face. The outlaw staggered back, blood pumping from a hole where his nose had been. He tried to keep upright and grabbed for the horse, becoming entangled in the traces. The horse panicked but could go nowhere with the dead weight of Sloane hindering it.

Hagerman's gunnies now joined in the fight, pulling weapons and shooting at the buckboard. A hail of fire swept across the vehicle, some shots going wide, others hitting the sides. Quigley felt a blow in his thigh, and he cursed and fired again at Hagerman, this time hitting him in the chest. Hagerman went down, and Quigley switched his fire to the gunmen. Beside him Noreen cried out as a bullet creased her arm. In a sudden blaze of anger she brought up her rifle, firing back at the group of gunnies.

Blane Golay had his revolver out and fired at Murray. The bullet went wide and hit Betsy in the neck. She screamed and grabbed at the wound as blood pumped on to her jacket.

'Damn you all!' Murray yelled, and jumped down out of the buckboard and into the street on the opposite side from the gunmen. He crouched behind the wheel and fired beneath the vehicle, taking Golay's legs out from under him. The gunman felt to the dirt and Murray pumped another two slugs into him. The outlaw rolled up in a ball and stayed that way.

Quigley emptied one Colt and snatched his second from the holster and continued firing almost without pause. Beside him Noreen was firing steadily – the noise of gunfire hideous in the quietness of the almost deserted town. A gunman turned and limped back towards the Red Nugget. Noreen put a bullet in him, and he threw up his hands and went down and stayed down. Suddenly there were no more targets. A silence fell over the street, broken only by the sound of a wounded gunnie moaning.

Murray climbed back into the seat beside Betsy, wincing as he felt the wound in his side pulling. Betsy was holding a bloodstained hand against her neck. He pulled off his bandana and offered it to her.

'Here, use that to staunch the blood. We need to get you to a doctor.'

'I think it's just a nick,' she said. 'The bleeding seems to be easing.' She noticed how he favoured his side. 'You've been hit.'

'Ain't much. I guess I'll live. Quigley, are you all right?'

'I got one in the leg,' he called back and turned to Noreen and saw the blood on her arm. 'Noreen's hit. She's bleeding. Here, let me bind that.'

'What about you?' she queried, noting his blood-soaked leg.

'Murray, can you get the buggy rolling and take us to the sawbones. Looks like we all caught some lead.'

'Sure thing, but Sloane is all tangled up in the traces. I'll have to get him free afore we go anywhere.'

Murray climbed down to pull the dead outlaw from the tangled reins, and then paused as he heard the sound of hoofbeats. The drumming grew louder, and into sight came the posse.

'Damn,' Murray muttered, 'just when a fella needed a break.'

The horsemen hauled up. Slater and his deputies were in the lead. They took in the bloody scene with dead men strewn across the width of the street – and suddenly an awful lot of guns were pointing at the people in the buckboard.

'You men there,' Slater shouted, 'throw down your guns. Otherwise we'll blow you to kingdom come.'

152

35

They were caught flat-footed. Quigley knew that one false move on their part and the twitchy members of the posse would start shooting. Even now it was touch and go. And then Huston McRae appeared at the entrance of the Red Nugget. Behind him came his brother, and both had guns aimed across the street at the buckboard.

'All right,' Quigley yelled. 'Don't shoot. We give up.'

'Keep your hands where we can see them and step away from the wagon,' Slater called.

Quigley held up his gun, and in full sight placed it in the buckboard. He limped into the roadway, followed by Murray, favouring his side where he had been wounded.

'The women too!' McRae shouted when he saw Noreen and Betsy were making no attempt to get down from the buckboard.

'Leave the women out of this,' Quigley said. 'You just want me. Let everyone else go.'

He had moved so he was standing by McRae's straw boss, lying in the dirt, a bullet-riddled corpse.

'The hell you say,' McRae retorted. 'They drove that coach into the crowd and now my son is badly injured. They'll hang alongside you.'

'Wait a minute,' someone called, 'you can't hang no women.'

'Who's to tell me what I can do and what I can't do?' snarled McRae. 'Fetch the ropes and let's get on with the hanging. I want this done today. Then we can all come back here and enjoy a drink. Every man jack at the hanging is entitled to free drinks for as long as he can stand upright.'

There was the rumble of muttering from the posse members.

'Hell, I signed up to hunt those two varmints, not hanging females,' a big bearded man said. He was turning his horse away. 'Count me out of this game.'

Some men were easing their horses away from the body of the posse. But McRae stepped down into the street, raised his gun and fired it in the air. The shot frightened some of the horses, and they jittered about while the riders tried to calm them. In the confusion some men took the opportunity to slip away.

'When this is all over,' McRae roared, 'I'll blacklist all those men as welched on me.'

There was more grumbling amongst the riders, but in spite of McRae's threat, more and more were disappearing into alleyways, the posse thinning out even as McRae watched. These men might be beholden to Huston McRae in some fashion, but the thought of hanging a woman was too much for most.

It was while McRae was distracted by the recalcitrance in his townsmen that Quigley saw his chance. All eyes were on the rancher as he stood fuming impotently in the street waving his gun at the crowd and cussing them for cowardly dogs. Quigley dropped on one knee beside the body of a gunman and snatched the gun that had fallen from the dead man's hand.

'McRae,' he yelled. 'Drop that gun. I got you dead to rights.'

But Huston McRae was no coward, and no slouch with a gun. These days he hired men to do his killing for him, but he had been a capable gunman in his time. He swivelled and fired off a shot at the man challenging him. The bullet hit Quigley in the shoulder. He grunted, and ignoring the pain, shot back at McRae, hitting him in the gut. McRae staggered back, firing off another round that went somewhere over Quigley's head. Quigley pumped another bullet into McRae, and the rancher sat down in the dirt.

Behind the stricken town boss, Slater and his deputies, seeing what was happening, were trying to bring their weapons to bear on Quigley, kneeling in the street. But they were hindered by their nervous horses, already spooked by McRae's first shot, and the further gunfire set them to plunging and fighting their bits. Packed close together in the confines of the street it wasn't easy for their riders to bring them under control.

Behind Quigley, Murray had also grabbed up a weapon from one of the dead men, and began firing at Slater's lawmen. Quigley was in the dirt scrabbling for another weapon dropped by the men he had killed, and then he, too, was firing at the posse.

In the buggy Noreen was staring across at Justin McRae standing on the boardwalk, his gun in his hand. She saw him aim at the men in the street. Noreen had kept hold of her rifle while she waited to see what would come of Quigley's plea to leave her and Betsy alone. McRae got off one shot. Noreen didn't know where that one went, but it was enough to make her raise her rifle.

'Drop the gun, Justin,' she yelled.

But either he did not hear her, or he chose to ignore her – she was never to know. He fired again, and Quigley jerked as the bullet hit him. Noreen hesitated no longer, but pulled the trigger, the rifle resting on the side of the buggy keeping it steady. The heavy bullet punched Justin McRae backwards. He cannoned into the saloon doors and disappeared from sight. Numbed from what she had just done, Noreen froze where she was and stared at the doors swinging back and forth on their hinges.

Quigley was lying on his side, trying to bring up his gun, but his vision blurred. He felt the vibration of hoof beats as he lay pressed into the dirt. His gun clicked on empty and he tossed it aside. He tried to get his eyes to work, looking for another weapon. A pair of boots approached. He gazed up, trying to make out who it was. Sheriff Slater stood over him. Somewhere in the background was the vibration of a body of horses on the move.

'Damn you, Quigley,' the sheriff spluttered, tears in his eye. 'You shot McRae. Now I aim to kill you.'

The revolver was raised, and Quigley had enough vision to see the little black eye of the gun centred on him. The sound of the shot made him wince. Slater staggered back, a baffled look on his face. He looked up and saw Murray with a smoking revolver in his hand – tried to pull the trigger of his gun, but Murray blasted out another shot. The lawman went down heavily, the way a dead man goes down.

'Quigley!' Murray's strong arms were around him, lifting him. 'Don't you go and die on me, Quigley.'

Then there were more horsemen in the street – many riders and people shouting commands, ordering everyone to throw down their weapons.

'Murray,' Quigley whispered, 'I'm sorry. Sorry I got you into this.'

A figure loomed over them. Quigley knew then that he had died. Judge Leyman Updegrove was standing in the street glaring down at him.

EPILOGUE

Quigley made his way out of the courtroom on crutches, his wounds still troubling him. By his side was his deputy Murray, and behind them came Noreen, her arm in a sling and Betsy wearing a scarf around her neck to conceal the bandage. The street was crowded with noisy townsfolk discussing the court proceedings.

Judge Updegrove had presided over the coroner's court, convened to establish the facts of the events that had left a dozen or more people dead in the streets of Slimwater. Two men came out behind the little group – Marshal Thamon Wattles and Marshal Everet Koder.

'Quigley!' Wattles called.

Quigley turned his head and stared at the marshal who had refused to accompany them into Slimwater on the stagecoach, and had taken his and Murray's horses and deserted them. Wattles was smiling, but there was no corresponding smile on Quigley's face.

'Huh!'

'Just wanted to congratulate you on the outcome of the court,' Wattles said effusively. 'Judge Updegrove was right in saying what a fine job you did in cleaning up this rats' nest you found here in Slimwater.'

He held out his hand. Quigley looked down at his own hands grasping his crutches.

'Just a moment, Marshal. Murray, would you hold these for me?'

Murray took the crutches. Quigley balled his fists and slung a haymaker at the grinning marshal. It was a good punch, completely taking the lawman by surprise. The stricken man stumbled back and went down.

'That's for stealing my horse.'

'Son of a bitch!' Wattles yelled.

There was blood on his mouth. He grabbed for his gun, and that was when Murray stepped in and smashed the crutch across his hand, knocking the weapon to the ground.

'You're a coward and a disgrace to the badge,' Quigley fumed. 'I've recommended the judge kick you off the marshals' registrar.'

'I'll get you for this, Quigley,' Wattles shouted. 'No man does that to me and lives.'

'Any time, Wattles, any time. Right now I ain't armed. Just say the word and face me man to man out here on the street. But that wouldn't be your style, would it? You'd want to shoot me in the back.'

The downed man glared sullenly back at Quigley, who turned to Murray and reached for his crutches.

'Come on, let's get out of here. The smell of skunk is mighty rank just now.'

The little party continued into the street, Murray grinning all over his face.

'Right, you two,' Betsy said, moving to Quigley's side and linking her arm in his. 'You are coming out to the ranch where we can keep an eye on you. Noreen, grab that other big galoot. It seems to me these two get into trouble when left to their own devices. Also they look like they need feeding up a mite.'

Shortly the little party were seated in the buckboard. As they drove out of Slimwater, Jemima was perched on Murray's knee, talking animatedly while the big man sat listening attentively. Gradually the buckboard was lost to view as it headed out to the Barrel B.

Library Link Issues (For Staff Use Only)

1	2	3	4	5	6	7	8	9